The Haunted Hills

The Haunted Hills

Ghost Tales of Ireland for Children

Chosen by Joan Ryan and Gordon Snell

GLENDALE PRESS

First published in Ireland by
THE GLENDALE PRESS
18 Sharavogue
Glenageary Road Upper
Dun Laoghaire
Co. Dublin, Ireland

ISBN 0 907606 20 2

Cover and Book Design by Q
Typeset by Print Prep (Ireland) Ltd
Printed by Mount Salus Press, Dublin

Contents

Acknowledgements

The editors and publishers gratefully acknowledge the following sources: Mr. Mervyn Wall and the Talbot Press Ltd. for 'The Demon Angler' from *A Flutter of Wings*, 1974; Dr. Caoimhín Ó Danachair and the Mercier Press Ltd. for 'The Midnight Mass' from *Folk Tales of the Irish Countryside*, 1967; Mr. Gerard Murphy and Browne and Nolan Ltd. for 'Godfather Death' from *Tales from Ireland*, 1947; Mr. Douglas Sealy for 'The Friars of Urlaur' by Douglas Hyde from *Legends of Saints and Sinners;* the publishers of *Our Boys* for 'Squire Walter's Duel', 1927; Mr. Sean O'Sullivan and B.T. Batsford Ltd. for 'Dead Couple Marry after Death' and 'Midnight Funeral from America' from *Legends from Ireland*, 1977.

Grateful acknowledgement is also given to the following sources for illustrative material: *Pictures from Punch* 1891; *Instant Archive Art*, The Graphic Communications Centre Ltd., Kent; *Illustrated London News*; *1800 Woodcuts by Thomas Berwick and his School*, edited by B. Cirker, Dover Publications, New York.

In the event of any copyright holders having been overlooked the publishers will be only too pleased to come to an arrangement at the first available opportunity.

Introduction

Whether or not you really believe in ghosts, you can meet plenty of them in the old stories; and the tales chosen for this collection show their amazing variety.

Here you'll find a headless horse and rider, challenging a living horseman to a race; a phantom wedding, and a duel of the dead; a haunted lake, a cavern full of ghostly warriors, and even a see-through coach-and-horses.

Other stories tell how the skeletons made music at Daniel Crowley's party, how a priestly spirit said Mass in a ruined church, and how the Tinker of Ballingarry vanquished the devil himself. There are tricksters, pipers with magic powers, and a black boar that dances on water.

Like the stories in our other collections, *Land of Tales* and *Sea-Tales of Ireland*, these stories come from many sources. A number of them are from the oral tradition, passed on from one generation to another; some appeared in magazines and journals; others are original stories, or old tales re-told by modern writers.

All of them are the kind of stories that can be read to yourself, or read aloud — especially if you want to feel that pleasant tingle of fear, as a ghostly tale is told in the flickering firelight, while the wind whistles outside, and who knows what spirits are roaming abroad. . . .

Joan Ryan and Gordon Snell

FOR LEONARD AND MAEVE
WITH MUCH LOVE

John Connors and The Fairies

by JEREMIAH CURTIN

There was a man named John Connors, who lived near Killarney, and was the father of seven small children, all daughters and no sons. Connors fell into such rage and anger at having so many daughters, without any sons, that when the seventh daughter was born he would not come from the field to see the mother or the child.

When the time came for christening he wouldn't go for sponsors, and didn't care whether the wife lived or died. A couple of years after that a son was born to him, and some of the women ran to the field and told John Connors that he was the father of a fine boy. Connors was so delighted that he caught the spade he had with him and broke it on the ditch. He hurried home then and sent for bread and meat, with provisions of all kinds to supply the house.

'There are no people in the parish,' said he to the wife, 'fit to stand sponsors for this boy, and when night comes I'll ride over to the next parish and find sponsors there.'

When night came he bridled and saddled his horse, mounted, and rode away toward the neighbouring parish to invite a friend and his wife to be godfather and godmother to his son. The village to which he was going was Beaufort, south of Killarney. There was a public-house on the road. Connors stepped in and treated the bystanders, delayed there a while, and then went his way. When he had gone a couple of miles he met a stranger

11

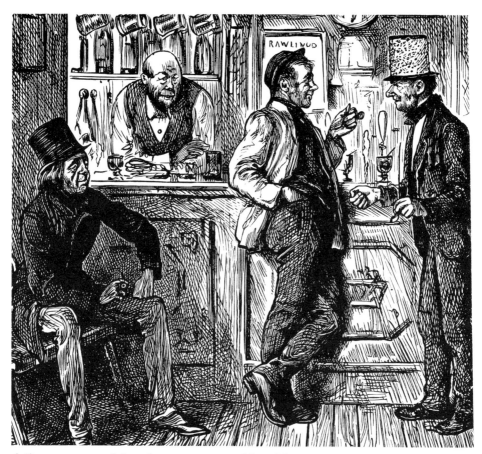

riding on a white horse, a good-looking gentleman wearing red knee-breeches, swallow-tailed coat, and a tall hat.

The stranger saluted John Connors, and John returned the salute. The stranger asked where was he going at such an hour.

'I'm going,' said Connors, 'to Beaufort to find sponsors for my young son.'

'Oh, you foolish man,' said the stranger; 'you left the road a mile behind you. Turn back and take the left hand.'

John Connors turned back as directed, but never came to a cross-road. He was riding about half an hour when he met the same gentleman, who asked: 'Are you the man I met a while ago going to Beaufort?'

'I am.'

'Why, you fool, you passed the road a mile or more behind. Turn back and take the right hand road. What trouble is on you that you cannot see a road when you are passing it?'

Connors turned and rode on for an hour or so, but found no side road. The same stranger met him for the third time, and asked him the same question, and told him he must turn back. 'But the night is so far gone,' said he, 'that you'd better not be waking people. My house is near by. Stay with me till morning. You can go for the sponsors to-morrow.'

John Connors thanked the stranger and said he would go with him. The stranger took him to a fine castle then, and told him to dismount and come in.

'Your horse will be taken care of,' said he, 'I have servants enough.'

John Connors rode a splendid white horse, and the like of him wasn't in the country round. The gentleman had a good supper brought to Connors. After supper he showed him a bed and said, 'Take off your clothes and sleep soundly till morning.'

When Connors was asleep the stranger took the clothes, formed a corpse just like John Connors, put the clothes on it, tied the body to the horse, and leading the beast outside, turned its head towards home. He kept John Connors asleep in bed for three weeks.

The horse went towards home and reached the village next morning. The people saw the horse with the dead body on its back, and all thought it was the body of John Connors. Everybody began to cry and lament for their neighbour. He was taken off the horse, stripped, washed, and laid out on the table. There was a great wake that night, everybody mourning and lamenting over him, for wasn't he a good man and the father of a large family? The priest was sent to celebrate mass and attend the funeral, which he did. There was a large funeral.

Three weeks later John Connors was roused from his sleep by the gentleman, who came to him and said:

'It is high time for you to be waking. Your son is christened. The wife, thinking you would never come, had the child baptized, and the priest found sponsors. Your horse stole away from here and went home.'

'Sure then I am not long sleeping?'

'Indeed, then, you are: it is three whole days and nights that you are in that bed.'

John Connors sat up and looked around for his clothes, but if he did he could not see a stitch of them. 'Where are my clothes?' asked he.

'I know nothing of your clothes, my man, and the sooner you go out o' this the better.'

Poor John was astonished. 'God help me, how am I to go home without my clothes? If I had a shirt itself, it wouldn't be so bad; but to go without a rag at all on me!"

'Don't be talking,' said the man; 'take a sheet and be off with yourself. I have no time to lose on the like of you.'

John grew in dread of the man, and taking the sheet, went out. When well away from the place he turned to look at the castle and its owner, but if he did there was nothing before him but fields and ditches.

The time as it happened was Sunday morning, and Connors saw at some distance down the road people on their way to mass. He hurried to the fields for fear of being seen by somebody. He kept to the fields and walked close to the ditches till he reached the side of a hill, and went along by that, keeping well out of sight. As he was nearing his own village at the side of the mountain there happened to be three or four little boys looking for stray sheep. Seeing Connors, they knew him as the dead man buried three weeks before. They screamed and ran away home, some of them falling with fright. When they came to the village they cried that they had seen John Connors, and he with a sheet on him.

Now, it is the custom in Ireland when a person dies to sprinkle holy water on the clothes of the deceased and then give them to poor people or to friends for God's sake. It is thought that by giving the clothes in this way the former owner has them to use in the other world. The person who wears the clothes must wear them three times to mass one Sunday after another and sprinkle them each time with holy water. After that they may be worn as the person likes.

When the women of the village heard the story of the boys some of them went to the widow and said:

''Tis your fault that your husband's ghost is roaming around in nakedness. You didn't give away his clothes.'

'I did, indeed,' said the wife. 'I did my part, but it must be that the man I gave them to didn't wear them to mass, and that is why my poor husband is naked in the other world.'

Now she went straight to the relative and neighbour who got the clothes. As she entered the man was sitting down to breakfast.

'Bad luck to you, you heathen!' said she. 'I did not think you the man to leave my poor John naked in the other world. You neither went to mass in the clothes I gave you nor sprinkled holy water on them.'

'I did, indeed. This is the third Sunday since John died, and I went to mass this morning for the third time. Sure I'd be a heathen to keep a relative naked in the other world. It wasn't your husband that the boys saw at all.'

She went home then, satisfied that everything had been done as it should be.

An uncle of John Connors lived in the same village. He was a rich farmer and kept a servant girl and a servant boy. The turf bog was not far away, and all the turf at the house being burned, the servant girl was told to go down to the reek and bring home a creel of turf. She went to the reek and was filling her creel, when she happened to look towards the far end of the reek, and there she saw a man sticking his head out from behind the turf, and he with a sheet on him. She looked a second time and saw John Connors. The girl screamed, threw down the creel, and ran away, falling every few steps from terror. It was to the reek that Connors had gone, to wait there in hiding till dark. After that he could go to his own house without any one seeing him.

The servant girl fell senseless across the farmer's threshold, and when she recovered she said: 'John Connors is below in the bog behind the reek of turf, and nothing but a sheet on him.'

The farmer and the servant boy laughed at her and said: 'This is the way with you always when there's work to do.'

The boy started off to bring the turf himself, but as he was coming near the reek John Connors thrust his head out, and the boy ran home screeching worse than the girl. Nobody would go near the reek now, and the report went out that John Connors was below in the bog minding the turf. Early that evening John Connors' wife made her children go on their knees and offer up the rosary for the repose of their father's soul. After the rosary they went to bed in a room together, but were not long in it when there was a rap at the door. The woman asked who was outside. John Connors answered that it was himself.

'May the Almighty God and His blessed Mother give rest to your soul!' cried the wife, and the children crossed themselves and covered their heads with the bed-clothes. They were in dread he'd come in through the keyhole; they knew a ghost could do that if it wished.

John went to the window of two panes of glass and was tapping at that. The poor woman looked out, and there she saw her husband's face. She began to pray again for the repose of his soul, but he called out:

"Bad luck to you, won't you open the door to me or throw out some clothes? I am perishing from cold.'

This only convinced the woman more surely. John didn't like to break the door, and as it was strong, it wouldn't be easy for him to break it, so he left the house and went to his uncle's. When he came to the door all the family were on their knees repeating the rosary for the soul of John Connors. He knocked, and the servant girl rose up to see who was outside. She unbolted and unlatched the door, opened it a bit, but seeing Connors, she came near

cutting his nose off, she shut it that quickly in his face. She bolted the door then and began to scream: 'John Connors' ghost is haunting me! Not another day or night will I stay in the house if I live to see morning!'

All the family fastened themselves in in a room and threw themselves into bed, forgetting to undress or to finish their prayers. John Connors began to kick the door, but nobody would open it; then he tapped at the window and begged the uncle to let him in or put out some clothes to him, but the uncle and children were out of their wits with fear.

The doctor's house was the next one, and Connors thought to himself, 'I might as well go to the doctor and tell all to him; tell him that the village is gone mad.' So he made his way to the doctor's, but the servant boy there roared and screeched from terror when he saw him, ran to his master, and said, 'John Connors' ghost is below at the door, and not a thing but a sheet on him.'

'You were always a fool,' said the doctor. 'There is never a ghost in this world.'

'God knows, then, the ghost of John Connors is at the door,' said the boy.

To convince the boy, the master raised the upper window. He looked out and saw the ghost sure enough. Down went the window with a slap.

'Don't open the door!' cried the doctor. 'He is below; there is some mystery in this.'

Since the doctor wouldn't let him in any more than the others, John Connors was cursing and swearing terribly.

'God be good to us,' said the doctor. 'His soul must be damned, for if his soul was in purgatory it is not cursing and swearing he'd be, but praying. Surely, 'tis damned he is, and the Lord have mercy on the people of this village; but I won't stay another day in it; I'll move to the town to-morrow morning.'

Now John left the doctor's house and went to the priest, thinking that he could make all clear to the priest, for everybody else had gone mad. He knocked at the priest's door and the house-keeper opened it. She screamed and ran away, but left the door open behind her. As she was running towards the stairs she fell, and the priest, hearing the fall, hurried out to see what the matter was.

'Oh, Father,' cried the house-keeper, 'John Connors' ghost is below in the kitchen, and he with only a sheet on him!'

'Not true,' said the priest. 'There is never a person seen after parting with this world.'

The words were barely out of his mouth when the ghost was there before him.

'In the name of God,' said the priest, 'are you dead or alive? You must be dead, for I said mass in your house, and you a corpse on the table, and I was at your funeral.'

'How can you be foolish like the people of the village? I'm alive. Who would kill me?'

'God, who kills everybody, and but for your being dead, how was I to be asked to your funeral?'

''Tis all a mistake,' said John. 'If it's dead I was it isn't here I'd be talking to you to-night.'

'If you are alive, where are your clothes?'

'I don't know where they are or how they went from me, but I haven't them, sure enough.'

'Go into the kitchen,' said the priest. 'I'll bring you clothes, and then you must tell me what happened to you.'

When John had the clothes on he told the priest the day the child was born he went to Beaufort for sponsors, and, being late, he met a gentleman, who sent him back and forth on the road and then took him to his house. 'I went to bed,' said John, 'and slept till he waked me. My clothes were gone from me then, and I had nothing to wear but an old sheet. More than this I don't know: but everybody runs from me, and my wife won't let me into the house.'

'Oh, then, it's Daniel O'Donohue, King of Lochlein, that played the trick on you,' said the priest. 'Why didn't you get sponsors at home in this parish for your son as you did for your daughters? For the remainder of your life show no partiality to son or daughter among your children. It would be a just punishment if more trouble came to you. You were not content with the will of God, though it is the duty of every man to take what God gives him. Three weeks ago your supposed body was buried and all thought you dead through your own pride and wilfulness.'

'That is why my wife wouldn't let me in. Now, your Reverence, come with me and convince my wife, or she will not open the door.'

The priest and John Connors went to the house and knocked, but the answer they got was a prayer for the repose of John Connors' soul. The priest went to the window then and called out to open the door.

Mrs. Connors opened the door, and seeing her husband behind the priest she screamed and fell: a little girl that was with her at the door dropped speechless on the floor. When the woman recovered, the priest began to persuade her that her husband was living, but she wouldn't believe that he was alive till she took hold of his hand: then she felt his face and hair and was convinced.

When the priest had explained everything he went away home.

No matter how large his family was in after years, John Connors never went from home to find sponsors.

(from *Tales of the Fairies and of the Ghost World*)

The Friars of Urlaur

by DOUGLAS HYDE

In times long ago there was a House of Friars on the brink of Loch Urlaur but there is nothing in it now except the old walls, with the water of the lake beating up against them every day in the year that the wind be's blowing from the south.

Whilst the friars were living in that house there was happiness in Ireland, and many is the youth who got good instructions from the friars in that house, who is now a saint in heaven.

It was the custom of the people of the villages to gather one day in the year to a 'pattern,' in the place where there used to be fighting and great slaughter when the Firbolgs were in Ireland, but the friars used to be amongst the young people to give them a good example and to keep them from fighting and quarrelling. There used to be pipers, fiddlers, harpers and bards at the pattern, along with trump-players and music-horns; young and old used to be gathered there, and there used to be songs, music, dancing and sport amongst them.

But there was a change to come and it came heavy. Some evil spirit found out its way to Loch Urlaur. It came at first in the shape of a black boar, with tusks on it as long as a pike, and as sharp as the point of a needle.

One day the friars went out to walk on the brink of the lake. There was a chair cut out of the rock about twenty feet from the brink, and what should they see seated in the chair but the big black boar. They did not know what was in it. Some of them said that it was a great water-dog that was in it, but they were not long in doubt about it, for it let a screech out of it that was heard seven miles on each side of it; it rose up then on its hind feet and was there screeching and dancing for a couple of hours. Then it leaped into the water, and no sooner did it do that than there rose an awful storm which swept the roof off the friars' house, and off every other house within seven miles of the place. Furious waves rose upon the lake which sent the water twenty feet up into the air. Then came the lightning and the thunder,

and everybody thought that it was the end of the world that
was in it. There was such a great darkness that a person could
not see his own hand if he were to put it out before him.

The friars went in and fell to saying prayers, but it was not
long till they had company. The great black boar came in, opened
its mouth, and cast out of it a litter of bonhams. These began on
the instant running backwards and forwards and screeching as
loud as if there were the seven deaths on them with the hunger.
There was fear and astonishment on the friars, and they did not
know what they ought to do. The abbot came forward and desired
them to bring him holy water. They did so, and as soon as he
sprinkled a drop of it on the boar and on the bonhams they went
out in a blaze of fire, sweeping part of the side-wall with them
into the lake.

'A thousand thanks to God,' said the Father Abbot, 'the devil
is gone from us.'

But my grief! he did not go far. When the darkness departed
they went to the brink of the lake, and they saw the black boar
sitting in the stone chair that was cut out
in the rock.

'Get me my curragh,' said the Father
Abbot, 'and I'll banish the thief.'

They got him the curragh and holy
water, and two of them went into the
curragh with him, but as soon as they
came near to the black boar he leaped
into the water, the storm rose, and the
furious waves, and the curragh and the
three who were in it were thrown high
up upon the land with broken bones.

They sent for a doctor and for the
bishop, and when they told the story to
the bishop he said, 'There is a limb of
the devil in the shape of a friar amongst

you, but I'll find him out without delay.' Then he ordered them all to come forward, and when they came he called out the name of every friar, and according as each answered he was put on one side. But when he called out the name of Friar Lucas he was not to be found. He sent a messenger for him, but could get no account of him. At last the friar they were seeking for came to the door, flung down a cross that he had round his neck, smote his foot on it, and burst into a great laugh, turned on his heel, and into the lake. When he came as far as the chair on the rock he sat on it, whipped off his friar's clothes and flung them out into the water. When he stripped himself they saw that there was hair on him from the sole of his foot to the top of his head, as long as a goat's beard. He was not long alone, the black boar came to him from the bottom of the lake, and they began romping and dancing on the rock.

Then the bishop enquired what place did the rogue come from, and the Superior said that he came a month ago from the north, and that he had a friar's dress on him when he came, and that he asked no account from him of what brought him to this place.

'You are too blind to be a Superior,' said the bishop, 'since you do not recognise a devil from a friar.'

While the bishop was talking the eyes of everyone present were on him, and they did not feel till the black boar came behind them and the rogue that had been a friar riding on him.

'Seize the villain, seize him,' says the bishop.

'You didn't seize me yourself,' says the villain, 'when I was your pet hound, and when you were giving me the meat that you would not give to the poor people who were weak with the hunger; I thank you for it, and I'll have a hot corner for you when you leave this world.'

Some of them were afraid, but more of them made an attempt to catch the black boar and its rider, but they went into the lake, sat on the rock, and began screaming so loud that they made the bishop and the friars deaf, so that they could not hear one word from one another, and they remained so during their life, and that is the reason they were called the 'Deaf Friars,' and from that day to this the old saying is in the mouth of the people, 'You're as deaf as a friar of Urlaur.'

The black boar gave no rest to the friars either by night or day: he himself, and the rogue of a companion that he had, were persecuting them in many a way, and neither they themselves nor the bishop were able to destroy or banish them.

At last they were determining on giving up the place altogether, but the bishop said to them to have patience till he would take counsel with Saint Gerald, the patron saint of Mayo. The bishop went to the saint and told him the story from beginning to end.

'That sorrowful occurence did not take place in my county,' said the saint, 'and I do not wish to have any hand in it.'

At this time Saint Gerald was only a higher priest in Tirerrill but anything he took in hand succeeded with him, for he was a saint on earth from his youth. He told the bishop that he would be in Urlaur, at the end of the week, and that he would make an attempt to banish the evil spirit.

The bishop returned and told the friars what Gerald had said, and that message gave them great courage. They spent that week saying prayers, but the end of the week came, and another week went by, and Saint Gerald did not come, for 'not as is thought does it happen.' Gerald was struck with illness as it was fated for him, and he could not come.

One night the friars had a dream, and it was not one man alone

who had it, but every man in the house. In the dream each man saw a woman clothed in white linen, and she said to them that it was not in the power of any man living to banish the evil spirit except of a piper named Donagh O'Grady who is living at Tavraun, a man who did more good, says she, on this world than all the priests and friars in the country.

On the morning of the next day, after the matin prayers, the Superior said, 'I was dreaming, friars, last night about the evil spirit of the lake, and there was a ghost or an angel present who said to me that it was not in the power of any man living to banish the evil spirit except of a piper whose name was Donagh O'Grady who is living at Tavraun, a man who did more good in this world than all the priests and friars in the country.'

'I had the same dream too,' says every man of them.

'It is against our faith to believe in dreams,' says the Superior, 'but this was more than a dream, I saw an angel beside my white linen.'

'Indeed I saw the same thing,' says every man of them.

'It was a messenger from God who was in it,' said the Superior, and with that he desired two friars to go for the piper. They went to Tavraun to look for him and they found him in a drinking-house half drunk. They asked him to come with them to the Superior of the friars at Urlaur.

'I'll not go one foot out of this place till I get my pay,' says the piper. 'I was at a wedding last night and I was not paid yet.'

'Take our word that you will be paid,' said the friars.

'I won't take any man's word; money down, or I'll stop where I am.' There was no use in talk or flattery, they had to return home again without the piper.

They told their story to the Superior, and he gave them money to go back for the piper. They went to Tavraun again, gave the money to the piper and asked him to come with them.

'Wait till I drink another naggin; I can't play hearty music till I have my enough drunk.'

'We won't ask you to play music, it's another business we have for you.'

O'Grady drank a couple of naggins, put the pipes under his oxter and said, 'I'm ready to go with ye now.'

'Leave the pipes behind you,' said the friars, 'you won't want them.'

'I wouldn't leave my pipes behind me if it was to Heaven I was going,' says the piper.

When the piper came into the presence of the Superior, the Superior began examining him about the good works he had done during his life.

'I never did any good work during my life that I have any remembrance of,' said the piper.

'Did you give away any alms during your life?' said the Superior.

'Indeed, I remember now, that I did give a tenpenny piece to a daughter of Mary O'Donnell's one night. She was in great want of the tenpenny piece, and she was going to sell herself to get it, when I gave it to her. After a little while she thought about the mortal sin she was going to commit, she gave up the world and its temptations and went into a convent, and people say that she passed a pious life. She died about seven years ago, and I heard that there were angels playing melodious music in the room when she was dying, and it's a pity I wasn't listening to them, for I'd have the tune now!'

'Well,' said the Superior, 'there's an evil spirit in the lake out-side that's persecuting us day and night, and we had a revelation from an angel who came to us in a dream, that there was not a man alive able to banish the evil spirit but you.'

'A male angel or female?' says the piper.

'It was a woman we saw,' says the Superior, 'she was dressed in white linen.'

'Then I'll bet you five tenpenny pieces that it was Mary O'Donnell's daughter was in it,' says the piper.

'It is not lawful for us to bet,' says the Superior, 'but if you banish the evil spirit of the lake you will get twenty tenpenny pieces.'

'Give me a couple of naggins of good whiskey to give me courage,' says the piper.

'There is not a drop of spirits in the house,' says the Superior, 'you know that we don't taste it at all.'

'Unless you give me a drop to drink,' says the piper, 'go and do the work yourself.'

They had to send for a couple of naggins, and when the piper drank it he said that he was ready, and asked them to show him the evil spirit. They went to the brink of the lake, and they told him that the evil spirit used to come on to the rock every time that they struck the bell to announce the 'Angel's Welcome.'

'Go and strike it now,' says the piper.

The friars went, and began to strike the bell, and it was not long till the black boar and its rider came swimming to the rock. When they got up on the rock the boar let a loud screech, and the rogue began dancing.

The piper looked at them and said, 'Wait till I give ye music.' With that he squeezed on his pipes, and began playing, and on the moment the black boar and its rider leapt into the lake and made for the piper. He was thinking of running away, when a great white dove came out of the sky over the boar and its rider, shot

31

lightning down on top of them and killed them. The waves threw them up on the brink of the lake, and the piper went and told the Superior and the friars that the evil spirit of the lake and its rider were dead on the shore.

They all came out, and when they saw that their enemies were dead they uttered three shouts for excess of joy. They did not know then what they would do with the corpses. They gave forty tenpenny pieces to the piper and told him to throw the bodies into a hole far from the house. The piper got a lot of tinkers who were going the way and gave them ten tenpenny pieces to throw the corpses into a deep hole in a shaking-scraw a mile from the house of the friars. They took up the corpses, the piper walked out before them playing music, and they never stopped till they cast the bodies into the hole, and the shaking-scraw closed over them and nobody ever saw them since. The 'Hole of the Black Boar' is to be seen still. The piper and the tinkers went to the public house, and they were drinking till they were drunk, then they began fighting, and you may be certain that the piper did not come out of Urlaur with a whole skin.

The friars built up the walls and the roof of the house and passed prosperous years in it, until the accursed foreigners came who banished the friars and threw down the greater part of the house to the ground.

The piper died a happy death, and it was the opinion of the people that he went to Heaven, and that it may be so with us all!

(from *Legends of Saints & Sinners*)

The Tinker of Ballingarry and his Three Wishes

by JEREMIAH CURTIN

In Ballingarry, County Limerick, there lived once a tinker named Jack. All tinkers are poor, and so was Jack; still he was not so poor as another, for he had a small garden behind his cottage and a fine apple tree in it. Jack travelled the country nearly all the time and left his wife to mind the cottage and garden.

One day while on the road with his pack he met a very 'dacent' looking man and saluted him respectfully. The stranger was pleased with the tinker, and said:

'Three wishes will be given you. You can ask for three things. You will get whatever you ask for. Do the best you can. You will never have a chance like this again.'

Jack thought and said: 'I have a strong old armchair in my house. Whoever comes in sits down in that chair and I have to stand. I wish now every one who sits on the chair from this out to grow fast to it, and the chair to be fast to the ground, and no man to have power to rise from the chair till I say the word.'

'Granted,' said the man. 'Now

tell your second wish, and 'tis my advice to you to wish for something that will be of service — something that will do you good.'

Jack thought awhile and said: 'In my garden is a tree which bears beautiful apples, but all the small boys and little blackguards of the country steal every apple of them and I never have one to eat. I wish every person who tries to steal an apple from that tree to be fastened to the apple and the apple to the tree and to have the person hung there till freed by me.'

'Granted,' said the man. 'Now is your third and last chance. I advise you for the last time. Wish for something of service. Be careful and get what will be of use to you.'

Jack thought, and thought, and then said:

'My wife has a leather bag: in that bag she puts scraps of wool that the neighbours give her when she works for them. Now, the small boys and little blackguards of the country come to my house, kick this bag around, pull the wool out and waste it. I wish everything that goes into the bag to stay in it till I give the word to go out.'

'Granted,' said the man, 'but, my poor fellow, you have done ill for yourself.'

The fine-looking gentleman went his way travelling, and Jack, the tinker, went home happy, but as poor as before.

Some time after Jack met with an accident, and lay at home a whole year. He was at death's door from hunger, when a stranger walked the way one day and said to him:

'I see, my good man, that you are very poor and in need. You are hungry. I am ready to make a bargain with you. I will give you comfort and make a rich man of you if you will come with me at the end of seven years.'

'Your offer is very enticing. Who are you?' asked Jack.

'Who am I?' repeated the stranger. 'To make a long story short, I'm the Devil.'

'No matter, your honour, who you are. I'll take your offer.' And Jack promised to be ready to go with the stranger at the end of seven years.

The Devil went away, and Jack was very rich for a tinker. There was no lack of food in his house: there was plenty from that out, and to spare. He went tinkering no longer from place to place, or if he did itself it was for his own pleasure. His wife went wool-picking for the neighbours no longer. They remained in their cottage, and all went well with the tinker and his wife, to the great surprise of the people around.

Jack soon forgot the Devil and the promise that he had given him. The seven years passed quickly; the last day of the last year came, and the stranger stood before Jack.

'The seven years are up,' said he. 'Come with me; I have done my part, now you must do yours.'

'A promise is a promise,' said Jack. 'I'll go with you; I am well satisfied. But do you sit in this chair awhile, and wait for me: I'll not delay long. As I am leaving the wife forever, I'd like to say a last word to her. I'll be back in a minute and go with you.'

The Devil sat down in Jack's chair, and waited. Jack was not long in giving good-bye to the wife, and said: 'I am ready; let us start.'

The Devil tried to rise, but, pull and jerk as he might, he could not move from the chair nor stir the chair from the ground. He let a screech out of him that was heard over three townlands, and struggled terribly, but no use for him, he could not rise. Seeing that he was fast and that there was no escape for him, he said to Jack: 'I'll give you twice as much wealth and fourteen years to enjoy it in if you will release me.'

'I am satisfied,' said Jack. 'Up and away with you.'

The Devil shot away like a dart of lightning. Now Jack was twice as rich as before, but he made no show of his wealth. He lived in the same little cottage.

The fourteen years passed as quickly as the seven, for Jack had twice as much to spend. The time was up again, and the Devil was at the front door. He was very watchful this time, and said to the tinker:

'You'll play me no tricks now. Get ready and come.'

Jack made ready quickly. The day was hot, and when they were ready to start, Jack said:

'We may as well go through my garden. Many is the pleasant hour I spent in it. Now that I am never to pass another day there, I would like a last look at the place.'

The Devil consented, sure of Jack this time. They walked through the garden to the end of it, where there was a large tree loaded with beautiful apples.

'The day is hot,' said Jack, 'the journey before us a long one. You are taller than I. Pluck some of those nice apples; they will be good on the road.'

'I will do that same,' said the Devil, and springing, he caught a large apple, but he could neither pull off the apple nor loosen his hold on it. There he was, swinging from the tree. He shouted and screeched, struggled and pulled, but no use for him.

'Take me down out of this,' said he.

'Indeed, then, I will not; you may stay there till the day of judgment, for anything I care.'

'You'll have no luck in your house if you leave me here,' said the Devil.

'Luck or no luck,' said Jack, 'I'd rather have you there than go with you.'

'Well,' said the Devil at last, 'I will give you three times the wealth you had at first and twenty-one years to enjoy it in if you will loosen me.'

Jack thought a while, and then said to himself: 'It is better to let him off than to have him here near me. He might do me some harm though he is in the tree.' So Jack freed the Devil from the apple tree, and away he went without delay.

Jack had wealth and plenty for twenty-one years; whatever he wished for he had. At the end the Devil stood before him and said: 'You'll play me no trick this turn, and when I have you in my kingdom I'll pay you for what you have done to me; I'll be even with you there.'

'I'll have to take my chances with you, I suppose,' said Jack, 'but let me say good-bye to my wife now.'

'Very well,' said the Devil.

Jack went to his wife, took the wool bag, and started. The two walked forward quickly. Jack was silent a long time; at last he said to the Devil: 'I have been thinking of the time when I was a little boy and the children of the village and I used to play a trick together. I was very nimble in those days, but now I am old and heavy. I brought this bag with me to remind me of my boyhood.'

He took out the bag, and, showing it to the Devil, said:

'I used to jump in and out of this bag, I was so quick and active.'

'Oh, what sort of a trick is that?' said the Devil. 'That's no trick at all.'

'Well,' said Jack, 'I don't think you can do it, and I'll never believe you can till I see you.'

He held the bag open; the Devil sprang in. Jack closed the bag in an instant, and said:

'Now you are in and I'll never let you out.'

In spite of the howling inside Jack put the bag on his back and went on. The Devil begged and begged.

'Oh, let me out,' cried he to Jack, but Jack would not listen to him.

In a couple of hours the tinker came to a place where four men were thrashing grain with flails.

'I have a bag here that's too thick and stiff to carry. Will you give it a few blows? Make it limber for me,' said he.

The men walloped the bag. It hopped like a ball. They flailed it till they broke their flails.

'Take that bag out of this,' cried the men. 'The Devil himself must be in it.'

'Oh, then,' said Jack, 'maybe it's himself that's in it, sure enough.'

He travelled on with the bag on his shoulders; the Devil was begging and promising at every step of the journey.

'No,' said Jack, 'I'll never let you out again to do harm in the world. I will pay you for your work.'

Jack found a tucking mill, and going to the owner, said: 'I want to thicken this bag a little, will you let it go once through the mill?'

'Oh, why not,' said the man.

Jack threw the bag in; the man was surprised at the cracking and smashing and terrible noise in the bag. After a while what happened to the mill but to break.

'Out of that! I am beggared entirely; my mill is in bits. Out o' that with your bag, it must be the Devil that's in it!'

'Sure and maybe it's the truth you are telling,' said Jack, taking the bag and walking off with it.

After a while he came to a forge; four strong men were at work with four sledges on a great piece of iron.

'The day is hot,' said Jack, 'and my bag is weighty and stiff. Will you give it a few blows of the sledge for me?'

The men winked at one another, as much as to say, we'll make bits of the bag for him.

'Why not?' said they.

Jack threw down the bag; the four men went at it, gave it many a good blow; each time they struck the bag flew to the top of the forge. The men worked till tired and panting; then called out: 'Away with your bag; it must be the Devil himself that's in it!'

The foreman, angry at the loss of time and work, caught a pointed hot iron from the fire and punched the bag with it. The iron went into the Devil's eye and destroyed it. He howled and screamed.

'Let me out! Let me out! I promise never to come in your way. I will not have you in my kingdom. I'll leave you alone forever. I'll give you riches for four times as long as at first.'

At last Jack opened the bag and let him out. Away flew the Devil, and was soon out of sight.

Jack went home now a free man, with plenty to eat and drink

for twenty-eight years. But the twenty-eight years passed quickly, and Jack, being a tinker, could never save a penny. He was very old, and after the end of the twenty-eight years he was very poor. His day came at last and he went to the other world. He stood at the door of the good place and knocked.

'Go to the one you worked for all your life. You cannot come here,' was the answer.

Jack went and rapped at the gate of the bad place. They asked: 'Who is there?'

'Jack the tinker, from Ballingarry.'

'Oh, don't let him in!' screamed a voice: 'don't let him in! He put my eye out; he will destroy every one of us.'

There was fear and trembling at the sound of Jack's voice. He could get no admittance to that place at any price. The tinker went back then to the gate of the good place. He could not enter, but sentence was passed to let him travel the world forever and carry a small lantern at night. He was to have no rest, but wander over bogs, marshes, moors, and lonely places and lead people astray.

He is roaming and travelling, and will be in that way till the day of judgment.

People know him as Jack O'Lantern.

(from *Irish Folk Tales*)

Squire Walter's Duel

Twenty years have now passed since I spent the memorable Christmas of 1907 in distant Lisakeen. I was a university student then in Dublin, and during my early years there had found in Dudley Madden a true friend and admirable companion.

Dudley was the only son of Dr. Madden, of Lisakeen, in County Galway, who lived there with his daughter, Kathleen, then twenty-two, and a year her brother's senior.

Gladly accepting my companion's invitation, I packed up my traps and went with him to the West for the Christmas holidays.

Just two days before Christmas we departed from Dublin via the Broadstone on a heavily-laden train of home-comers, cattle-jobbers, and people who seem to live in trains. After a steady and fast run of two hours the train drew up at Ballinasloe. Jerry Lynch, the man of all work at the doctor's, was there to meet us with a cob and back-to-back gig, to face a ten miles drive.

Whipping up the horse, Jerry muttered that there was 'rale signs of a white Christmas at any rate.' After two weary hours on the road we whisked up the short avenue to Lisakeen House.

After the necessary introductions we all gathered together for dinner in the old-fashioned dining-room, where a huge fire of turf and oak crackled and blazed, flinging fantastic shadows on the panelled walls about us.

The meal passed merrily, the doctor being an excellent story-

teller and a great wit. At eleven the old man and his daughter retired, leaving Dudley and myself all alone by the smouldering fire.

'Of course,' said I, 'you have the family ghost or the family banshee, who are liable to be knocking about this time of the year.'

'Well, we haven't got either to my knowledge, but I have often heard the people around say they saw Walter Madden, my grand-uncle, leading the hunt by the old mill below,' my friend replied with a meek smile. 'He was master of the 'Blazers' years and years ago, and was killed at the church 'liss' in a duel with one Bob Kirwan, who disposed of his body and quitted the country. Jerry

48

says that poachers saw the ghostly reproduction of the duel in the same place on the last night of the old year some winters ago, but the whole yarn, in my belief, is a fake.'

'Could never tell,' I remarked, as I prepared to retire for the night.

Christmas slipped by quickly, and the last day of the old year dawned cold and frosty. The snow that had fallen earlier in the week had drifted and frozen by the walls and the hollows of the fields. Peace reigned supreme over the land as Dudley and I surveyed the white soft landscape from the dining-room window.

'Sorry to be leaving you for the day,' he remarked, 'but Dad says I must call over to the O'Kellys and invite them for to-morrow night, and his word is law. Perhaps you might be able to amuse yourself alone till I return. Try Clonwood in the evening for a pheasant — sure to get one about six,' he shouted back over his shoulder, and was gone.

Passing the short winter's day writing some letters, about half-five I shouldered my gun and endeavoured to persuade Sweep, the big setter, to accompany me for a shot. Sweep, however, seemed totally indisposed in that line, evidently preferring the hearth-rug to the snowy ground outside, and so I had to go alone. The evening wind whistled overhead, and the pine-tops moaned beneath its cold breath as I beat about in an open spot for the spurred monarch to rise.

Suddenly a whirring sound, a flutter of wings, and a beautiful cock pheasant rose ten paces in front. Bang, bang, went both barrels. The pheasant wavered, came nearer to earth, but still continued his flight at a good rate.

However, ten minutes later the dead champion lay in the bottom of my bag. I then retraced my steps towards Lisnakill, or the Church Liss as it was commonly called. Musing and dreaming to myself, I made my way gingerly along till I gained the church.

Click; something made a noise in front of me, right by the door-way in the gable, just as if some-body struck his foot on a loose stone. Raising my head and turning more fully towards the portal, I saw what well-nigh froze my blood.

A man of powerful build was standing there intently watching me. His attire was that usually worn by the horsemen of O'Connell's time, body-coat jacket, boots, high hat and spurs of glittering steel. A riding crop was clutched in his hand, and from a quaint old leathern belt hung a rapier. The man's face was furrowed and cruel, the eyes hard and glittering, the eyebrows a heavy black and knitted.

The moon was bright, and I recognised, not flesh and blood, but the frightful-looking ghost of the man in the dining-room picture — Walter Madden.

The hypnotic influence of his gaze paralysed my will-power, but enlivened my sense of perception. Rooted to the ground, I faced the glare of the ghost before me — the duellist, long ago called to give account of his earthly stewardship. He neither moved towards me nor backwards into the chapel, but, now and then, allowed his gaze to wander sideways, as if expecting to meet some phantom comrade of his past career.

The wind stirred the evergreens on the opposite wall, and, oh Heavens! I could see the very ivy through the man's body. Hearing a slight movement on my right, slowly the vision of a second man arose before me.

Similarly attired as Walter's ghost, the new arrival was a younger and more supple man than Squire Madden. The latter shifted his awful glassy stare from me to the newcomer, whom I surmised, on recollecting the story already told me, to be Kirwan.

Together both men moved out into the open plot and faced each other. Drawing their swords, they measured their distance, and again faced each other. Quick as lightning, the two ghosts rushed madly to the fray. I was about to witness a spirited rehearsal of a duel fought seventy years ago.

Kirwan's ghost was the abler of the two. Crossing swords, they twisted and bent their phantom forms; and it seemed one had his opponent conquered, and now, in turn, he was forced to retreat. With dexterous skill they parried and cross-cut, blocked and retaliated, never speaking a word, nought save the sharp noise of steel against steel breaking the uncanny stillness of the night.

51

For a long while the battle raged; the same unearthly glitter in their eyes, the same activity marking their backward and forward movements. Then, with one quick, noiseless rush, the younger duellist coupled in, and, in the twinkling of an eye, his cold steel blade had transfixed his stubborn antagonist.

Reeling, Squire Walter fell, and with outstretched finger pointed towards an old hollow oak-tree twenty yards away, his eyes mean-

while turned appealingly on me, as if he desired I should search in the tree for something he wanted.

Slowly from my sight he vanished into the air. I was dumb-founded. All fear had now left me — I stood like one in a trance. Slowly, too, the other ghost faded away, his face awfully pale, and a look of terror and hate in his stony eyes.

The nocturnal duel had ended.

I moved over to the gnarled old oak and swung myself up on the lowest limb, kicking away the growth of multicoloured frozen fungi that had collected round the hollow opening of the tree trunk.

An odour of mustiness pervaded the atmosphere. Lighting a match, I knelt on the branch and held the little torch down into the breach. Upright against the rotting bark lay a human skeleton, bare and repulsive, with myriads of cobwebs woven about the skull.

Not a particle of flesh or clothing adhered to the bones. An old leathern girdle enveloped the skeleton waist, from which a heavy rusty rapier was suspended.

Now fascinated more than afraid, match after match I lighted until at last inside the belt I discovered a worm-eaten old wallet that crumpled when I took it in my hand. Shoving it into my breast-pocket, I descended, took my gun, and half an hour later was again seated at the dining-room fire in Lisakeen House.

Telling in whispered conversation my strange experiences to Dudley, who had also just returned, we decided to conceal the whole thing from the Doctor and Kathleen.

'Open the old knapsack, or whatever you found,' said Dudley.

I opened it, and found nothing but a half-sheet of parchment-like paper, discoloured and almost threadbare with age and damp-ness. Holding it up to the light, in excited tones I read:—

Fearing for my personal safety, I hid here, in this tree, the body of Walter Madden, Lisakeen, whom I killed in a duel last night, and am leaving Ireland for ever to-day.

Vengeance of God is following me, and justice shall find me out. Whoever discovers the body, let him bury it in decent ground, and thus lighten the burden of sorrow on my soul.

I herein affix my signature,

ROBERT KIRWAN.

This 4th day of January, 1835.

So ended the strange epistle. The mystery of Walter Madden's and Bob Kirwan's disappearance was at last solved.

The following night Dudley and I buried all that was mortal of the Madden duellist.

(from Our Boys)

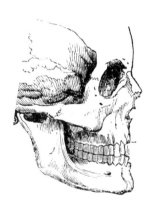

Dan Doolin's Ghost

by BARRY O'CONNOR

To give you my honest and candid opinion, I have very little faith in ghosts, but as we happen to be on the subject, I'll give you my experience in that line.

I was once coming home from the fair of Clonmel; I had two companions with me, Phil Brennan, a pig-jobber, and Joe Scanlan, a butter-and-egg merchant in a small way. The night was fine, with a bright moon shining through the green leaves over our heads, till we could almost see to pick up a pin. But before we were five miles on the road a sudden change came. The sky grew as black as pitch, and a tremendous rain-storm followed it. There was no place of shelter near at hand, so in a mighty time not one of us had a dry stitch to our backs.

It was a very lonely road, with nothing but trees on each side of us. After we got to what we found to be a fingerpost, we looked to the right and could spy something shining like a will o' the wisp, about half a mile from where we stood. We lost no time, but went in the direction of the light, and found to our glad surprise that it was coming from the window of Ned Ahearn's tavern; and I needn't tell you that we didn't leave the grass grow under our feet before we were snugly seated beside a big, blazing turf-fire inside the public house. And when we thought of the black storm raging without, and looked at the ruddy glow of the chimney corner within, it warmed our hearts, in spite of the wet clothes that were sticking to us, and with the help of a steaming jug of punch we

57

were soon beyond the reach of a cold.

After that we had a fine hearty supper of rashers and eggs. And maybe we didn't do justice to it sooner than give the house or the landlord a bad name. After supper we sat by the fireside with a few more travellers that put up there for the night like ourselves, and were amusing themselves before going to bed, telling stories about leprechauns, phookas, banshees, and such like. At last one of them said: 'Now, neighbours, if it pleases you, I'll tell you a ghost story.'

'A ghost story, indeed!' said another of the company, who looked like a scholar from Trinity College. He had a pale, boyish face, with large, staring eyes, and a head of long hair, falling

down his shoulders, as black as the ace of spades. 'Ghost stories,' said he, giving a melancholy smile, 'are fit only to amuse children — and tell me truly, did any of you ever see one? No, truth, I'll wager not. Can any man in this room stand up and honestly say that he believes in such nonsensical pisreoga?'

'Don't let your tongue wag so fast, young gentleman,' said a white-haired man with sun-burnt features, and as he stood up he looked as tall as a giant, and as straight as a pike-staff, he had the very cut of an old veteran. 'If you're too ignorant to believe in ghosts,' said he, 'that's no reason why you should insult the rest of the company by such remarks as you're just after making. Now, for my own part, I believe in such things, and I'm neither afraid nor ashamed to own it.'

'Then, all I can say is,' said the young scholar, 'that you look old enough to have more sense in your noddle.'

'What!' said the veteran, getting into a passion, 'do you mean to dispute the words of a man old enough to be your father?'

'It doesn't signify a rap to me,' said the scholar, 'if you were as old as the hills.'

'Oh, neighbours, do you hear this young sprig of impudence? Now, listen to me, my fine young dandy. I'll wager a ten pound note that I'll make you say you've seen a ghost before I've done with you.'

'Ten pounds!' said the scholar. 'I haven't that much money about me; if I had I'd soon take up your challenge, but maybe some of the rest of the company will take you at your word.'

'That's a mean way to slink out of it, after all your bragging a while ago. Now, listen, all of you,' said the veteran, 'I'll bet I can tell this clever young man what he's thinking about, and if that doesn't satisfy him, I'll make him admit to you all that he has seen a ghost.'

'This is all the cash I have,' said the young man, throwing a five-pound bank-note on the table. 'It's my last five pounds, but I'm willing to stake it that you can do no such thing.'

'And here's five more on top of it,' said I, covering his money with the five sovereigns I made at Clonmel that day.

'I'll not be behindhand, either,' said Phil Brennan, putting down his three one-pound notes, the whole of his day's profits.

'I'll not be outdone, either,' said Joe Scanlan, slapping down the last thirty shillings he had in the world.

'Is there any more?' said the old veteran, giving a dry grin as he threw the corner of his eye at the pile of gold and silver on the table. 'Well, there, that will cover all,' said he, putting down a roll of notes on the table. 'And now, neighbours, just watch how soon I'll put this young man through his drill.'

'Now begin,' said the young scholar, 'and tell what I'm thinking of.'

'Bedad, I will, and I hope it will please you,' said the veteran. 'But first, look at me straight in the eye — that's it. Now you want to know what it is you're thinking about?'

'I do,' said the scholar.

'Listen, then,' said the veteran.

'I'm all attention,' said the youth.

'Then, this is what your mind is on,' said the veteran; 'you're thinking about your bosom-friend and schoolmate, Dan Doolin; he that sailed for Australia three years ago. Am I right?'

'You are, truth,' said the scholar, turning as white as a sheet. 'What are you going to do next?'

'Keep your eye on me, and you'll soon learn,' said the veteran.

Striding up to the door that led into the landlord's kitchen, he then took out something like a match and struck it on the bowl of his clay pipe, and in a jiffy there was a big cloud of smoke round his head that hid his face entirely.

'Now,' said the veteran:

'Turn your head, and look at me,
And tell your neighbours what you see.'

'I see,' said the scholar, 'a heavy mist in front of me.'

'Don't move,' said the veteran, striking another match, and that minute there was another cloud of smoke of a lighter shade than the first. 'Now then,' said the veteran:

'Speak the truth and have no fear;
What you see let others hear.'

'I see something like outlines or the figure of a man, but the mist is too thick to discern the face.'

'Once more,' said the veteran, striking a third match, and all of a sudden there was a bright, golden cloud around the door where he stood.

'Now,' said he:

'Penetrate the golden light —
Convince all here that I was right.'

'What do you see now?'

'I see,' said the scholar, with a terrible cry, 'my poor friend, Dan Doolin, that lost his life three years ago in the Australian

bush. Yes, friends, it is the ghost of poor Dan. Don't take him from me; let my eyes rest on him. Dan — Dan — he's going — he's gone — poor Dan Doolin is gone!'

And the next minute, the young scholar was stretched on the broad of his back on the tavern floor in a fit, wailing and moaning like a banshee, and twisting and twining, till we thought every minute would be his last.

'I'll soon bring him to his senses,' said the veteran, with a jeering laugh.

'Get up, you poor, trembling spidogue,' said he, putting the scholar on his feet. 'You thought to defy and expose an old man to the contempt of the whole house tonight, but you see how neatly I've turned the laugh against you.'

'Hold him, friends, don't let him out of the house,' said the young man. 'He's a conjuror. Don't hinder me; let me at him!'

And the next minute he had his grip on the veteran's neck and dragged him up and down the room and around the table like a madman. But the cute old veteran in spite of his years, was too quick for him, for he gave one leap over the table and darted out through the door at his heels, and away the pair of them flew, pell-mell, through the thick woods, in the dead of the night. Such an exciting chase was never seen before nor since; but the strangest part of the story is

that both the veteran and scholar disappeared that night and were never seen again, either of them, from that hour to this.'

'And still,' said I, 'you say you have no faith in ghosts?'

'Neither I have; for the pair of scheming robbers swept every coin off the table before they took leg-bail, and left me a poorer man that night by five pounds. Phil Brennan bid good-bye to his three pounds, and Joe Scanlan never handled one farthing of his thirty shillings. So that the thimble-rigging vagabonds got safely away with nearly ten pounds for their night's diversion, and I suppose were laughing in their sleeves, thinking how cleanly they bamboozled us, with the help of Dan Doolin's ghost.

(from *Turf-Fire Stories and Fairy-Tales of Ireland*)

The Headless Horseman

Horseman

by T. CROFTON CROKER

G od speed you, and a safe journey this night to you, Charley,' ejaculated the master of the little sheebeen house at Ballyhooley after his old friend and good customer, Charley Culnane, who at length had turned his face homewards, with the prospect of as dreary a ride and as dark a night as ever fell upon the Blackwater, along whose banks he was about to journey.

Charley Culnane knew the country well, and, moreover, was as bold a rider as any Mallow boy that ever *rattled* a four-year-old upon Drumrue race-course. He had gone to Fermoy in the morning, as well for the purpose of purchasing some ingredients required for the Christmas dinner by his wife, as to gratify his own vanity by having new reins fitted to his snaffle, in which he intended showing off the old mare at the approaching St Stephen's day hunt.

Charley did not get out of Fermoy until late; for although he was not one of your 'nasty particular sort of fellows' in anything that related to the common occurrences of life, yet in all the appointments connected with hunting, riding, leaping, in short, in whatever was connected with the old mare, 'Charley,' the saddlers said, 'was the devil to *plase*.' An illustration of this fastidiousness was afforded by his going such a distance for a snaffle bridle. Mallow was full twelve miles nearer Charley's farm (which lay just three-quarters of a mile below Carrick) than Fermoy; but

Charley had quarrelled with all the Mallow saddlers, from hard-working and hard-drinking Tim Clancey, up to Mister Ryan, who wrote himself 'Saddler to the Duhallow Hunt;' and no one could content him in all particulars but honest Michael Twomey of Fermoy, who used to assert — and who will doubt it? — that he could stitch a saddle better than the lord-lieutenant, although they made him all as one as king over Ireland.

This delay in the arrangement of the snaffle-bridle did not allow Charley Culnane to pay so long a visit as he had at first intended to his old friend and gossip, Con Buckley, of the 'Harp of Erin.' Con, however, knew the value of time, and insisted upon Charley making good use of what he had to spare. 'I won't bother you waiting for water, Charley, because I think you'll have enough of that same before you get home; so drink off your liquor, man. It's as good *parliament* as ever a gentleman tasted, ay, and holy church too, for it will bear "x *waters*," and carry the bead after that, may be.'

Charley, it must be confessed, nothing loth, drank success to Con, and success to the jolly 'Harp of Erin,' with its head of beauty and its strings of the hair of gold, and to their better acquaintance, and so on, from the bottom of his soul, until the bottom of the bottle reminded him that Carrick was at the bottom of the hill on the other side of Castletown Roche, and that he had got no further on his journey than his gossip's at Ballyhooley, close to the big gate of Convamore. Catching hold of his oil-skin hat, therefore, whilst Con Buckley went to the cupboard for another bottle of 'the real stuff,' he regularly, as it is termed, bolted from his friend's hospitality, darted to the stable, tightened his girths, and put the old mare into a canter towards home.

The road from Ballyhooley to Carrick follows pretty nearly the course of the Blackwater, occasionally diverging from the river and passing through rather wild scenery, when contrasted with the beautiful seats that adorn its banks. Charley cantered gaily, regardless of the rain which, as his friend Con had anticipated, fell in torrents: the good woman's currants and raisins were carefully packed between the folds of his yeomanry cloak, which Charley, who was proud of showing that he belonged to the 'Royal Mallow Light Horse Volunteers,' always strapped to the saddle before him, and took care never to destroy the military effect of it by putting it on. — Away he went singing like a thrush —

> Sporting, belleing, dancing, drinking,
> Breaking windows — (*hiccup!*) — sinking;
> Ever raking — never thinking,
> Live the rakes of Mallow.

> Spending faster than it comes,
> Beating — (*hiccup, hic*), and duns,
> Duhallow's true-begotten sons,
> Live the rakes of Mallow.

Notwithstanding that the visit to the jolly 'Harp of Erin' had a little increased the natural complacency of his mind, the drenching of the new snaffle reins began to disturb him, and then followed a train of more anxious thoughts than ever were occasioned by the dreaded defeat of the pride of his long-anticipated *turn out* on St Stephen's day. In an hour of good fellowship, when his heart was warm, and his head not over cool, Charley had backed the old mare against Mr Jepson's bay filly Desdemona for a neat hundred, and he now felt sore misgivings as to the prudence of the match. In a less gay tone he continued

> Living short, but merry lives,
> Going where the devil drives,
> Keeping —

'Keeping' he muttered, as the old mare had reduced her canter to a trot at the bottom of Kilcummer Hill. Charley's eye fell on the old walls that belonged, in former times, to the Templars; but the silent gloom of the ruin was broken only by the heavy rain which splashed and pattered on the gravestones. He then looked up at the sky to see if there was, among the clouds, any hope for mercy on his new snaffle reins; and no sooner were his eyes lowered, than

his attention was arrested by an object so extraordinary as almost led him to doubt the evidence of his senses. The head, apparently, of a horse, with short cropped ears, large open nostrils, and immense eyes, seemed rapidly to follow him. No connection with body, legs, or rider, could possibly be traced — the head advanced — Charley's old mare, too, was moved at this unnatural sight, and, snorting violently, increased her trot up the hill. The head moved forward, and passed on; Charley pursuing it with astonished gaze, and wondering by what means, and for what purpose, this detached head thus proceeded through the air, did not perceive the corresponding body until he was suddenly startled by finding it close at his side. Charley turned to examine what was thus so sociably jogging on with him, when a most un-exampled apparition presented itself to his view. A figure, whose height (judging as well as the obscurity of the night would permit him) he computed to be at least eight feet, was seated on the body and legs of a horse full eighteen hands and a half high. In this measurement Charley could not be mistaken, for his own mare was exactly fifteen hands, and the body that thus jogged alongside he could at once determine, from his practice in horseflesh, was at least three hands and a half higher.

After the first feeling of astonishment, which found vent in the exclamation 'I'm sold now for ever!' was over, the attention of Charley, being a keen sportsman, was naturally directed to this extraordinary body, and having examined it with the eye of a connoisseur, he proceeded to reconnoitre the figure so unusually mounted, who had hitherto remained perfectly mute. Wishing to see whether his companion's silence proceeded from bad temper, want of conversational powers, or from a distaste to water, and the fear that the opening of his mouth might subject him to have it filled by the rain, which was then drifting in violent gusts against them, Charley endeavoured to catch a sight of his companion's face, in order to form an opinion on that point. But his vision failed in carrying him further than the top of the collar of the figure's coat, which was a scarlet, single-breasted hunting frock, having a waist of a very old-fashioned cut reaching to the saddle, with two huge shining buttons at about a yard distance behind. 'I ought to see further than this, too,' thought Charley, 'although he is mounted on his high horse, like my cousin Darby, who was made barony constable last week, unless 't is Con's whiskey that has blinded me entirely.' However, see further he could not, and after straining his eyes for a considerable time to no purpose, he exclaimed, with pure vexation, 'By the big bridge of Mallow, it is no head at all he has!'

'Look again, Charley Culnane,' said a hoarse voice, that seemed to proceed from under the right arm of the figure.

Charley did look again, and now in the proper place, for he clearly saw, under the aforesaid right arm, that head from which the voice had proceeded, and such a head no mortal ever saw before. It looked like a large cream cheese hung round with black puddings: no speck of colour enlivened the ashy paleness of the depressed features; the skin lay stretched over the unearthly surface, almost like the parchment head of a drum. Two fiery eyes of prodigious circumference, with a strange and irregular motion, flashed like meteors upon Charley, and a mouth that reached from either extremity of two ears, which peeped forth from under a profusion of matted locks of lustreless blackness. This head, which the figure had evidently hitherto concealed from Charley's eyes, now burst upon his view in all its hideousness. Charley, although a lad of proverbial courage in the county Cork, yet could not but feel his nerves a little shaken by this unexpected visit from the headless horseman, whom he considered this figure doubtless must be. The cropped-eared head of the gigantic horse moved steadily forward, always keeping from six to eight yards in

advance. The horseman, unaided by whip or spur, and disdaining the use of stirrups, which dangled uselessly from the saddle, followed at a trot by Charley's side, his hideous head now lost behind the lappet of his coat, now starting forth in all its horror as the motion of the horse caused his arm to move to and fro. The ground shook under the weight of its supernatural burden, and the water in the pools was agitated into waves as he trotted by them.

On they went — heads without bodies, and bodies without heads. The deadly silence of night was broken only by the fearful clattering of hoofs, and the distant sound of thunder, which rumbled above the mystic hill of Cecaune a Mona Finnea. Charley, who was naturally a merry-hearted, and rather a talkative fellow, had hitherto felt tongue-tied by apprehension, but finding his companion showed no evil disposition towards him, and having become somewhat more reconciled to the Patagonian dimensions of the horseman and his headless steed, he plucked up all his courage, and thus addressed the stranger —

'Why, then, your honour rides mighty well without the stirrups!'

'Humph!' growled the head from under the horseman's right arm.

''Tis not an over-civil answer,' thought Charley; 'but no matter, he was taught in one of them riding-houses, may be, and thinks nothing at all about bumping his leather breeches at the rate of ten miles an hour. I'll try him on the other tack. 'Ahem!' said Charley, clearing his throat, and feeling at the same time rather daunted at this second attempt to establish a conversation. 'Ahem! that's a mighty neat coat of your honour's, although 't is a little too long in the waist for the present cut.'

'Humph!' growled again the head.

This second humph was a terrible thump in the face to poor Charley, who was fairly bothered to know what subject he could start that would prove more agreeable. ''Tis a sensible head,' thought Charley, 'although an ugly one, for 't is plain enough the man does not like flattery.' A third attempt, however, Charley was determined to make, and having failed in his observations as to the riding and coat of his fellow-traveller, thought he would just drop a trifling allusion to the wonderful headless horse, that was jogging on so sociably beside his old mare; and as Charley was considered about Carrick to be very knowing in horses, besides being a full private in the Royal Mallow Light Horse Volunteers, which were every one of them mounted like real Hessians, he felt rather sanguine as to the result of his third attempt.

'To be sure, that's a brave horse your honour rides,' recommenced the persevering Charley.

'You may say that, with your own ugly mouth,' growled the head.

Charley, though not much flattered by the compliment, nevertheless chuckled at his success in obtaining an answer, and thus continued:

'May be your honour wouldn't be after riding him across the country?'

'Will you try me, Charley?' said the head, with an inexpressible look of ghastly delight.

'Faith, and that's what I'd do,' responded Charley, 'only I'm afraid, the night being so dark, of laming the old mare, and I've every halfpenny of a hundred pounds on her heels.'

This was true enough, Charley's courage was nothing dashed at the headless horseman's proposal; and there never was a steeple-chase, nor a fox-chase, riding or leaping in the country, that Charley Culnane was not at it, and foremost in it.

'Will you take my word,' said the man who carried his head

so snugly under his right arm, 'for the safety of your mare?'

'Done,' said Charley; and away they started, helter skelter, over everything, ditch and wall, pop, pop, the old mare never went in such style, even in broad daylight: and Charley had just the start of his companion, when the hoarse voice called out 'Charley Culnane, Charley, man, stop for your life, stop!'

Charley pulled up hard.

'Ay,' said he, 'you may beat me by the head, because it always goes so much before you; but if the bet was neck and neck, and that's the go between the old mare and Desdemona, I'd win it hollow!'

It appeared as if the stranger was well aware of what was passing in Charley's mind, for he suddenly broke out quite loquacious.

'Charley Culnane,' says he 'you have a stout soul in you, and are every inch of you a good rider. I've tried you, and I ought to know; and that's the sort of man for my money. A hundred years it is since my horse and I broke our necks at the bottom of Kilcummer hill, and ever since I have been trying to get a man that dared to ride with me, and never found one before. Keep, as you have always done, at the tail of the hounds, never baulk a ditch, nor turn away from a stone wall, and the headless horseman will never desert you nor the old mare.'

Charley, in amazement, looked towards the stranger's right arm, for the purpose of seeing in his face whether or not he was in earnest, but behold! the head was snugly lodged in the huge pocket of the horseman's scarlet hunting-coat. The horse's head had ascended perpendicularly above them, and his extraordinary companion rising quickly after his avant courier, vanished from the astonished gaze of Charley Culnane.

Charley, as may be supposed, was lost in wonder, delight, and perplexity; the pelting rain, the wife's pudding, the new snaffle — even the match against squire Jepson — all were forgotten; nothing could he think of, nothing could he talk of, but the headless horseman. He told it, directly that he got home, to Judy; he told it the following morning to all the neighbours; and he told it to the hunt on St Stephen's day: but what provoked him after all the pains he took in describing the head, the horse, and the man, was that one and all attributed the creation of the headless horseman to his friend Con Buckley's 'X water parliament.' This, however, should be told, that Charley's old mare beat Mr Jepson's bay filly, Desdemona, by Diamond, and Charley pocketed his cool hundred; and if he didn't win by means of the headless horseman, I am sure I don't know any other reasons for his doing so.

(from *Fairy Legends and Traditions of the South of Ireland*)

The Ghost of the Valley

by LORD DUNSANY

I went for a walk one evening under old willows whose pollard-ed trunks leaned over a little stream. A mist lay over the stream and filled the valley far over the heads of the willows and hid the feet of the hills. And higher than that I saw a pillar of mist stand up from the rest, its head above the level of the grass slopes, where they ended under the edge of the darkening woods. So strange it seemed standing there in the dim of the evening, that I moved nearer to see it, which I could not clearly do where I was, nearly a hundred yards away, because of the rest of the

mist; but as I moved towards it, and less and less of the river-mist was between us, I saw it clearer and clearer, till I stood at the feet of that tall diaphanous figure.

One by one lights appeared where there had been none before: for it was that hour when the approach of night is noticed in cottages, and the flower-like glow of windows here and there was adding a beauty and mystery to the twilight. In the great loneliness there, with no-one to speak to, standing before that towering figure of mist that was as lonely as I, I should have liked to have spoken to it. And then there came to me the odd thought. Why not? There was no one to hear me, and it need not answer.

So I said 'What are you?' and so small and shrill was the answer, that at first I thought it was birds of the reeds and water that spoke. 'A ghost,' it seemed to be saying. 'What?' said I. And then more clearly it said, 'Have you never seen ghosts before?'

I said that I never had, and it seemed to lose interest in me. To regain its attention if possible, I said that I had sometimes seen queer things in the twilight which very likely were ghosts, although I did not know it at the time. And there seemed to come back into the tall grey figure some slight increase of intensity, as though its lost interest were slowly returning, and in tones that sounded scornful of my ignorance it said 'They probably were.'

'And you?' I inquired again.

'The ghost of this valley,' it said.

'Always?' I asked.

'Not always,' it said. 'Little more than a thousand years. My father was the smoke from one of those cottages and my mother was the mist over the stream. She of course was here always.'

It was strange to hear so tall a figure talking with so tiny a voice: had a waterhen been uttering its shrill cry near me it would have drowned the voice of the ghost, which barely emerged from the chatter of waterfowl farther away.

'What was it like in this valley,' I asked, 'when you were young?'

For a while the tall shape said nothing, and seemed to be

indolently turning its head, as though it looked from side to side of the valley. 'The heads of the willows were not cut,' it said. 'But that was when I was very young. They were cut off soon after. And there were not so many cottages. Not nearly so many, and they were all of thatch at first. They lit their fires in the evenings all through the autumn. My mother loved the autumn: it is to us what spring is to you. My father rose up then from one of the chimneys, high over the thatch, and the wind drifted him and so they met. He remembered the talk of the firesides long ago, but only a few centuries more than a thousand years. My mother can remember for ever. She remembers when there were no huts here and no men. She remembers what was, and knows what is coming.'

'I don't want to hear about that,' I said.

Something like a cackle of laughter seemed to escape from the ghost. But it may have been only the quacking of far-off ducks, which were flighting at that hour.

'What do you do yourself?' I asked.

'I drift,' it said, 'whenever there is a wind. Like you.'

'Drift!' I said. 'We don't drift. We have our policies.' I was about

to explain them to the ghost, when it interrupted.

'You all drift before them helplessly,' it said. 'You and your friends and your enemies.'

'It is easy for you to criticize,' I answered.

'I am not criticizing,' it said. 'I am just as helpless. I drift this way and that upon any wind. I can no more control the winds than you can turn Destiny.'

'Nonsense,' I said. 'We are masters of all Creation. We have made inventions which you would never understand down there by your river and the smoke of the cottages.'

'But you have to live with them,' it said.

'And you?' I asked.

'I am going,' it said.

'Why?' I asked it.

'Times are changing,' it said. 'The old firesides are altering, and they are poisoning the river, and the smoke of the cities is unwholesome, like your bread. I am going away among unicorns, griffons and wyverns.'

'But are there such things?' I asked.

'There used to be,' it replied.

But I was growing impatient at being lectured to by a ghost, and was a little chilled by the mist.

'Are there such things as ghosts?' I asked then.

And a wind blew then, and the ghost was suddenly gone.

'We used to be,' it sighed softly.

(from *The Third Ghost Book*)

The Enchantment of Gearóid Iarla

by PATRICK KENNEDY

In old times in Ireland there was a great man of the Fitzgeralds. The name of him was Gerald, but the Irish, that always had a great liking for the family, called him *Gearóid Iarla* — Earl Gerald. He had a great castle or rath at Mullaghmast, and whenever the English government were striving to put some wrong on the country, he was always the man that stood up for it. Along with being a great leader in a fight, and very skilful at all weapons, he was deep in the black art, and could change himself into whatever shape he pleased. His lady knew that he had this power, and often asked him to let her into some of his secrets, but he never would gratify her.

She wanted particularly to see him in some strange shape, but he put her off and off on one pretence or other. But she wouldn't be a woman if she hadn't perseverance, and so at last he let her know that if she took the least fright while he'd be out of his normal form, he would never recover till many generations of men would be under the mould. 'Oh!' She wouldn't be a fit wife for Gearóid Iarla if she could be easily frightened. Let him but gratify her in this whim, and he'd see what a hero she was!' So one beautiful summer evening, as they were sitting in their grand drawing room, he turned his face away from her, and muttered some words, and while you'd wink he was clever and clean out of sight, and a lovely goldfinch was flying about the room.

The lady, as courageous as she thought herself, was a little

83

startled, but she held her own pretty well, especially when he came and perched on her shoulder, and shook his wings, and put his little beak to her lips, and whistled the delightfullest tune

you ever heard. Well, he flew in circles round the room, and played hide and go seek with his lady, and flew out into the garden, and flew back again, and lay down in her lap as if he was asleep, and jumped up again.

Well, when the thing had lasted long enough to satisfy both, he took one more flight into the open air, but by my word he was soon on his return. He flew right into his

84

lady's bosom, and the next moment a fierce hawk was after him. The wife gave one loud scream, though there was no need, for the wild bird came in like an arrow and struck against a table with such force that the life was dashed out of him. She turned her eyes from his quivering body to where she saw the goldfinch an instant before, but neither goldfinch nor Earl Gerald did she ever lay eyes on again.

Once every seven years the Earl rides round the Curragh of Kildare on a steed, whose silver shoes were half an inch thick the time he disappeared, and when these shoes are worn as thin as a cat's ear, he will be restored to the society of living men, fight a great battle with the English, and reign King of Ireland for two score years.

Himself and his warriors are now sleeping in a long cavern under the Rath of Mullaghmast. There is a table running along through the middle of the cave. The Earl is sitting at the head, and his troopers down along in complete armour both sides of the table, and their heads resting on it. Their horses, saddled and bridled, are standing behind their masters in their stalls at each side; and when the day comes, the miller's son that's to be born with six fingers on each hand will blow his trumpet, and the horses will stamp and whinny, and the knights awake and mount their steeds, and go forth to battle.

Some night that happens once in every seven years, while the Earl is riding around the Curragh, the entrance may be seen by anyone chancing to pass by. About a hundred years ago, a horse-dealer that was late abroad and a little drunk, saw the lighted cavern, and went in. The lights, and the stillness, and the sight of the men in armour cowed him a good deal, and he became sober. His hands began to tremble, and he let fall a bridle on the pavement. The sound of the bit echoed through the long cave, and one of the warriors that was next to him lifted his head a little, and said in a deep hoarse voice, 'Is it time yet?' He had the wit to say, 'Not yet, but soon will,' and the heavy helmet sunk down on the table. The horse-dealer made the best of his way out, and I never heard of any other one getting the same opportunity.

(from *Legendary Fictions of the Irish Celts*)

The Ghost and his Wives

by WILLIAM LARMINIE

There was a man coming from a funeral, and it chanced as he was coming along by the churchyard he fell in with the head of a man. 'It is good and right,' said he to himself, 'to take that with me and put it in a safe place.'

He took up the head and laid it in the churchyard. He went on along the road home, and he met a man with the appearance of a gentleman.

'Where were you?' said the gentleman.

'I was at a funeral, and I found the head of a man on the road.'

'What did you do with it?' said the gentleman.

'I took it with me, and left it in the churchyard.'

'It was well for you,' said the gentleman.

'Why so?' said the man.

'That is my head,' said he, 'and if you did anything out of the way to it, assuredly I would be even with you.'

'And how did you lose your head?' said the man.

'I did not lose it at all, but I left it in the place where

you found it to see what you would do with it.'

'I believe you are a good person' (*i.e.* a ghost), said the man; 'and, if so, it would be better for me to be in any other place than in your company.'

'Don't be afraid, I won't touch you. I would rather do you a good turn than a bad one.'

'I would like that,' said the man. 'Come home with me till we get our dinner.'

They went home together.

'Get up,' said the man to his wife, 'and make our dinner ready for us.'

The woman got up and made dinner ready for them.

When they ate their dinner — 'Come,' said the man, 'till we play a game of cards.'

They were playing cards that evening, and he (the gentleman) slept that night in the house; and on the morning of the morrow they ate their breakfast together. When two hours were spent, —

'Come with me,' said the gentleman.

'What business have you with me?' said the man.

'That you may see the place I have at home.'

They got up and walked together till they came to the church-yard.

'Lift the tombstone,' said the gentleman.

He raised the tombstone and they went in. 'Go down the stairs,' said the gentleman.

They went down together till they came to the door; and it was opened, and they went into the kitchen. There were two old women sitting by the fire.

'Rise,' said the gentleman to one of them, 'and get dinner ready for us.'

She rose and took some small potatoes.

'Have you nothing for us for dinner but that sort?' said the gentleman.

'I have not,' said the woman.

'As you have not, keep them.'

'Rise you,' said he to the second wo-man, 'and get ready dinner for us.'

She rose and took some meal and husks.

'Have you nothing for us but that sort?'

'I have not,' said she.

'As you have not, keep them.'

He went up the stairs and knocked at a door. There came out a beautiful woman in a silk dress, and it ornamented with gold from the sole of her foot to the crown of her head. She asked him what he wanted. He asked her if she could get dinner for himself and the stranger. She said she could. She laid a dinner before them fit for a king. And when they had eaten and drunk plenty, the gentleman asked if he knew the reason why she was able to give them such a dinner.

'I don't know,' said the man; 'but tell me if it is your pleasure.'

'When I was alive I was married three times, and the first wife I had never gave anything to a poor man except little potatoes; and she must live on them herself till the day of judgment. The second wife, whenever any one asked alms of her, never gave anything but meal and husks; and she will be no better off herself, nor any one else who asks of her, till the day of judgment. The third wife, who got the dinner for us — she could give us everything from the first.'

'Why is that?' said the man.

'Because she never spared of anything she had, but would give it to a poor man; and she will have of that kind till the day of judgment.'

'Come with me till you see my dwelling,' said the gentleman.

There were outhouses and stables and woods around the house; and, to speak the truth, he was in the prettiest place the man ever saw with his eyes.

'Come inside with me,' said he to the man; and the man was not long within when there came a piper, and he told him to play, and he was not long playing when the house was filled with men and women. They began dancing. When part of the night was spent, the man thought he would go and sleep. He arose and went to sleep; and when he awoke in the morning he could see nothing of the house or anything in the place.

(from *West Irish Folk-Tales and Romances*)

Godfather Death

by GERARD MURPHY

Con O'Leary was looking for a godfather for his child. None of those that offered themselves satisfied him; for he found them partial and apt to favour their friends at the expense of others. Finally, a tall thin man came to the door.

'I hear you are looking for a god-father for your child,' said the tall thin man.

'I am,' said the father. 'But I'll have nobody partial or unfair. Who are you?'

'My name is Death,' said the tall thin man.

'If you're Death,' said the father, 'I need look no further. For there is no one so impartial as Death. You strike them all alike, without fear or favour. Will you be godfather to my child?'

'I will,' said Death. And the child was baptized.

'Now, you've done me an honour,' said Death, 'and I'll tell you something in return that may help you. Whenever you go to a sick person's bedside you'll see me in the room. If I am at the sick person's head, the sick person will die; but if I am at the sick person's feet, the sick person will recover.'

A few days later, Con O'Leary heard that a neighbour was ill. He went to visit him. He asked the woman of the house how her husband was.

'He's badly, Con,' said the woman of the house.

'Might I see him?' Con asked.

'I'm afraid not,' said the woman. 'The priest and the doctor have been here, and they said that no one should be let visit him.'

'If he's as bad as that, I'm all the more anxious to see him,' said Con. 'Would you mind telling him I'm here?'

The woman told her husband that Con O'Leary had arrived and was very anxious to speak to him. 'Send him in,' said the sick man.

Con went in. 'You're welcome, Con,' said the sick man.

'Long life to you,' said Con. 'How do you feel yourself?'

'Very bad,' said the sick man. 'It won't be long till I'm dead.'

'You're not going to die this time,' said Con; for he had seen Death standing at the sick man's feet. 'Get a drink of whey,' said Con to the sick man's wife. The wife brought the whey. Con put his arm round the sick man's shoulders and helped him to sit up. 'Drink this,' he said, putting the whey to the sick man's lips.

The sick man drank the whey. 'You'll see that you'll be all right in a few days' time,' said Con. 'I'll come again myself to-morrow.'

The next day, Con came again to the sick man's house.

'You are welcome, Con,' said the woman of the house. 'He's much better to-day.'

'Put out your tongue,' said Con to the sick man. 'It is my opinion,' said Con after he had examined the sick man's tongue, 'that you'll be doing your work as well as ever you were before a week is out.'

Con was right in his opinion, and soon everyone was saying that Con O'Leary was as good as any doctor and better than most.

A rich lord, who lived ten miles away, fell ill. He sent his coach to Con O'Leary's house to fetch him to his bedside.

'Oh! I couldn't go so far from home,' said Con, 'unless I were well paid for it.'

'You'll get whatever you ask,' said the coachman.

When Con came to the rich lord's bedside, he saw the tall thin man standing by his head. Con felt the sick man's pulse and looked at his tongue. 'You're as bad as a man could be,' he said.

'Is there no hope?' asked the lord.

Con thought for a few moments. 'You're lying the wrong way for your health,' he said. 'First we must turn you round the right way in the bed.' They moved the lord round in the bed so that his feet were where his head had been. Then Con went out to the garden and gathered some herbs. He made a cooling drink of the herbs and gave it to the sick man. The sick man began to feel better at once. That afternoon, he was able to sit up. He kept Con in the house for a week, treating him as he would a great doctor. He then paid him a large fee, and sent him home in the coach.

When Con arrived home, the tall thin man was waiting for him. 'No one can play tricks with Death,' said the tall thin man. 'You must come with me now.'

'Very well,' said Con; and they set off together. Death walked with him towards the sea. When they reached the sea, Con asked

Death for a few minutes' respite while he smoked his last pipe and drank his last drink. Death granted his request. Con took his pipe and a half-empty whiskey-bottle from his pocket. He offered Death a drink. Death drank some of the whiskey and Con drank what was left. They chatted while Con filled his pipe.

'My father was very clever at tricks,' said Con.

'What could he do?' asked Death.

'His best trick,' said Con, 'was jumping into a bottle no bigger than a whiskey-bottle.'

'That's easy,' said Death.

'Well, all I'll say,' said Con, 'is that it's something you could never do.'

'Show me the bottle,' said Death.

Con placed the bottle on the ground in front of Death. Death jumped into the bottle. When he was safely in, Con fixed the cork in the mouth of the bottle, and threw the bottle far out to sea.

For seven years no one died, for Death was closed up in the bottle being tossed about by the waves. At the end of seven years, the waves cast the bottle on the beach. A boy found it and drew out the cork. Death was free once more. He walked straight to Con O'Leary's house. This time Con O'Leary had to go. In spite of his cleverness, Death was too strong for him in the end.

(from *Tales from Ireland*)

Daniel Crowley and the Ghosts

by JEREMIAH CURTIN

There lived a man in Cork whose name was Daniel Crowley. He was a coffinmaker by trade, and had a deal of coffins laid by, so that his apprentice might sell them when he himself was not at home.

A messenger came to Daniel Crowley's shop one day and told him that there was a man dead at the end of the town, and to send up a coffin for him, or to make one.

Daniel Crowley took down a coffin, put it on a donkey cart, drove to the wakehouse, went in, and told the people of the house that the coffin was for them. The corpse was laid out on a table in a room next to the kitchen. Five or six women were keeping watch around it; many people were in the kitchen. Daniel Crowley was asked to sit down and commence to shorten the night — that

is, to tell stories, to amuse himself and the others. A tumbler of punch was brought, and he promised to do the best he could.

He began to tell stories and shorten the night. A second glass of punch was brought to him, and he went on telling tales. There was a man at the wake who sang a song; after him another was found, and then another. Then the people asked Daniel Crowley to sing, and he did. The song that he sang was of another nation. He sang about the good people, the fairies. The song pleased the company, who desired him to sing again, and he did not refuse.

Daniel Crowley pleased the company so much with his two songs that a woman who had three daughters wanted to make a match for one of them, and get Daniel Crowley as a husband for her. Crowley was a bachelor, well on in years, and had never thought of marrying.

The mother spoke of the match to a woman sitting next to her. The woman shook her head, but the mother said: 'If he takes one of my daughters, I'll be glad, for he has money laid by. Do you go and speak to him, but say nothing of me at first.'

The woman went to Daniel Crowley then, and told him that she had a fine, beautiful girl in view, and that now was his time to get a good wife; he'd never have such a chance again.

Crowley rose up in great anger. 'There isn't a woman wearing clothes I'd marry,' said he. 'There isn't a woman born that could bring me to make two halves of my loaf for her.'

The mother was insulted now and forgot herself. She began to abuse Crowley.

'Bad luck to you, you hairy little scoundrel,' said she, 'you might be a grandfather to my child. You are not fit to clean the shoes on her feet. You have only dead people for company day and night; 'tis by them you make your living.'

'Oh, then,' said Daniel Crowley, 'I'd prefer the dead to the living any day if all the living were like you. Besides, I have nothing against the dead. I am getting employment by them, and not by the living, for 'tis the dead that want coffins.'

'Bad luck to you, 'tis with the dead you ought to be, and not with the living; 'twould be fitter for you to go out of this altogether and go to your dead people.'

'I'd go if I knew how to go to them,' said Crowley.

'Why not invite them to supper?' retorted the woman.

He rose up then, went out, and called: 'Men, women, children, soldiers, sailors, all people that I have made coffins for, I invite you tonight to my house, and I'll spend what is needed in giving a feast.'

The people who were watching the dead man on the table saw him smile when he heard the invitation. They ran out of the room in a fright and out of the kitchen, and Daniel Crowley hurried away to his shop as fast as his donkey could carry him. On the way he came to a public-house, and, going in, bought a pint bottle of whiskey, put it in his pocket, and drove on.

The workshop was locked and the shutters down when he left that evening, but when he came near he saw that all the windows were shining with light, and he was in dread for the building or that robbers were in it. Then right there Crowley slipped into a corner of the building opposite, to know could he see what was happening, and soon he saw crowds of men, women, and children walking towards his shop and going in, but none coming out. He was hiding some time when a man tapped him on the shoulder and asked: 'Is it here you are, and we waiting for you? 'Tis a shame to treat company this way. Come now.'

Crowley went with the man to the shop, and as he passed the threshold he saw a great gathering of people. Some were neighbours, people he had known in the past. All were dancing, singing, amusing themselves. He was not long looking on when a man came up to him and said: 'You seem not to know me, Daniel Crowley.'

'I don't know you,' said Crowley. 'How could I?'

'You might then, and you ought to know me, for I am the first

man you made a coffin for, and 'twas I gave you the first start in business.'

Soon another came up, a lame man. 'Do you know me, Daniel Crowley?'

'I do not.'

'I am your cousin, and it isn't long since I died.'

'Oh, now I know you well, for you are lame. In God's name,' said Crowley to the cousin, 'how am I to get these people out of this? What time is it?'

''Tis early yet; it's hardly eleven o'clock, man.'

Crowley wondered that it was so early.

'Receive them kindly,' said the cousin; 'be good to them, make merriment as you can.'

'I have no money with me to get food or drink for them; 'tis night now, and all the places are closed,' answered Crowley.

'Well, do the best you can,' said the cousin.

The fun and dancing went on, and while Daniel Crowley was looking around, examining everything, he saw a woman in the far-

off corner. She took no part in the amusement, but seemed very shy in herself.

'Why is that woman so shy — she seems to be afraid?' asked he of the cousin. 'And why doesn't she dance and make merry like the others?'

'Oh, 'tis not long since she died, and you gave the coffin, as she had no means of paying for it. She is in dread lest you'll ask her for the money, or let the company know that she didn't pay,' said the cousin.

The best dancer they had was a piper by the name of John Reardon, from the City of Cork. The fiddler was one John Healy. Healy brought no fiddle with him, but he made one, and the way he made it was to take off what flesh he had on his body. He rubbed up and down on his own ribs, each rib having a different note, and he made the loveliest music that Daniel Crowley had ever heard. After that the whole company followed his example. All threw off what flesh they had on them and began to dance jigs and hornpipes in their base bones. When by chance they struck against one another in dancing, you'd think it was Brandon Mountain that was striking Mount Eagle, with the noise that was in it.

Daniel Crowley plucked up all his courage to know could he live through the night, but still he thought daylight would never

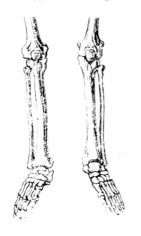

come. There was one man, John Sullivan, that he noticed especially. This man had married twice in his life, and with him came the two women. Crowley saw him taking out the second wife to dance a breakdown, and the two danced so well that the company were delighted, and all the skeletons had their mouths open, laughing. He danced and knocked so much merriment out of them all that his first wife, at the end of the house, became jealous and very mad, altogether. She ran down to where he was and told him she had a better right to dance with him than the second wife.

'That's not the truth for you,' said the second wife. 'I have a better right than you. When he married me you were a dead woman and he was free, and, besides, I'm a better dancer than what you are, and I will dance with him whether you like it or not.'

'Hold your tongue!' screamed the first wife. 'Sure, you couldn't come to this feast at all but for the loan of another woman's shinbones.'

Sullivan looked at his two wives, and asked the second one: 'Isn't it your own shinbones you have?'

'No, they are borrowed. I borrowed a neighbouring woman's shinbones from her, and 'tis those I have with me tonight.'

'Who is the owner of the shinbones you have under you,' asked the husband.

'They belong to one Catherine Murray. She hadn't a very good name in life.'

'But why didn't you come on your own feet?'

'Oh, I wasn't good myself in life, and I was put under a penalty, and the penalty is that whenever there is a feast or a ball I cannot go to it unless I am able to borrow a pair of shins.'

Sullivan was raging when he found that the shinbones he had been dancing with belonged to a third woman, and she not the best, and he gave a slap to the wife that sent her spinning into a corner.

The woman had relations among the skeletons present, and they were angry when they saw the man strike their friend. 'We'll never let that go with him,' said they. 'We must knock satisfaction out of Sullivan!'

The woman's friends rose up, and, as there were no clubs or weapons, they pulled off their left arms and began to slash and strike with them in terrible fashion. There was an awful battle in one minute.

While this was going on, Daniel Crowley was standing below at the end of the room, cold and hungry, not knowing but he'd be killed. As Sullivan was trying to dodge the blows sent against him, he got as far as Daniel Crowley, and stepped on his toes without knowing it. Crowley got vexed and gave Sullivan a blow with his fist that drove the head from him, and sent it flying to the opposite corner.

When Sullivan saw his head flying off from the blow, he ran, and, catching it, aimed a blow at Daniel Crowley with the head, and aimed so truly that he knocked him under the bench; then, having him at a disadvantage, Sullivan hurried to the bench and began to strangle him. He squeezed his throat and held him so firmly between the benches and the floor that the man lost his senses and couldn't remember a thing more.

When Daniel Crowley came to himself in the morning his apprentice found him stretched under the bench with an empty bottle under his arm. He was bruised and pounded. His throat was sore where Sullivan had squeezed it. He didn't know how the company broke up, nor when his guests went away.

(from *Tales of the Fairies and of the Ghost World*)

A Fisherman's Tale

A curious story is told in the North, which from the time that the incident of which it is the subject occurred, and the evidence of it that remain, seems entitled to some share of credit.

There was always a great plenty of bream in Lough M. till within the last sixty years, when they disappeared on a sudden, and though persons have constantly fished in the lake since, there has not been a single one taken, whilst perch and roach are caught in great abundance.

On inquiring from an old man, who lives close to the lake, the cause of this strange affair, he told me the following story.

For some years before the flight of the bream, there were two men named Morris and Brady, who constantly fished here. They knew every part of the lake, and had great success in taking the bream. For several years they agreed well enough, till some men set up a still in the adjoining bog. They persuaded Morris to give up his old employment and join with them in the still — but here, says the old man, the bad work begins.

It was not more than half a year after the still was set up, when some one informed against Morris and his friends, who shortly after saw their still and their all carried away by the guager. From this out Morris was seldom seen sober, and though he before gave good bread to his family, he now worked but seldom, spending the most of his time in a shebeen house.

Whilst Morris was thus becoming a beggar, Brady was getting prosperous, and was able to increase his stock with a cow, and to grow more flax than he used. His success made him hateful to Morris, who looked on with a wicked eye, and he would even sometimes tell his friends, that Brady informed and got money for it.

But to make a long story short, Morris with two others happened to go out to fish one night in the end of summer, and taking too much of the potheen, they began to quarrel with each other. One of them observing Brady, as he watched his lines seated in his cot, told his companions, who rowed up. They seemed to him at first friendly, but they shortly accused him of informing on them, which raised a fight, and whilst his companions were seizing on Brady, Morris took an oar and drove it through the bottom of the boat, which filled and sunk with Brady.

His two companions fled from the country, but Morris being taken was tried, yet for want of proof he was acquitted. He lived in this place for seven years after, and it was remarked that as often as he went on the water, the lake became disturbed and heaved the cots about as if it blew a storm, though the day itself was calm.

At length when Morris was dying, he called together his neighbours and told them the whole story, and, said he, 'no person can ever catch a bream, till all who were on the lake the night of

Brady's murder, are dead.'

As yet, says the old man, Morris's words are true, for one of his companions is, they say, alive in America, and in my memory, I never saw a bream come from the lake, though I have always lived beside it.

(from *The Dublin Penny Journal*)

The Midnight Mass

by KEVIN DANAHER

You know the old graveyard below at Ranasaer? Well, I'll tell you a queer thing that happened there.

A part of the old church is standing there yet, and the people used to say that a light would be seen in it from time to time, but they were all in dread of whatever might be in it, and no one would go near the place after dark.

There was a man that was strange to the place going past one night late. He was from the Dromcolliher side and he was walking home from Rathkeale after doing some business, and it was a bright moonlight night. He knew nothing about the old church ruin and he never heard any of the stories about it, and so, when he saw the lights inside — he could see that it was a churchyard — he said to himself that maybe it was grave robbers or something bad going on, and that he should take a look at whatever it was.

In with him across the field to the wall of the burying ground. It was all quiet, only the light burning inside in the ruin, and he could not see what it was, and so he went in over the wall without a sound and stole over to the window.

And there were two wax candles in sconces on the altar and the priest in his vestments. The Dromcolliher man could not make out what was going on until the priest turned around and said. 'Is there any one here who will answer my mass?' And the man outside says to himself that it is a queer time of the night to be saying mass, and a queer place too, but he supposed it was all right, and maybe that it was some new rule that a mass was to be said now and again in the old places where it used to be said before the English burned our old churches.

And with that he spoke up, and told the priest that he would serve the mass. And so he did: the priest said the mass and he gave the answers and did everything that the server does in the chapel on a Sunday.

And when it was finished the priest turned and spoke to him.

'Now I can rest in peace,' said the priest.

'Once a year,' said he, 'for more than two hundred years I am coming back here looking for some one to answer my mass. I was a priest in a religious order, and we were supposed to say a certain number of masses, and I neglected to say one of them. And one day the soldiers came and killed us all. And the other priests that had their duty done, were let into heaven, but I could not get in until I had said that mass, and a living person would have to witness it. And I am thankful to you. And go your road now in safety,' says he, and he lifting his hand the way a priest gives you his blessing. And the man got up from his knees.

'Good night to you, Father, and God bless you!' says he, and away out to the road with him.

And when he looked back there was not a sign of the light or the priest to be seen, only the moonlight shining on the old ruin.

(from *Folk Tales of the Irish Countryside*)

Dead Couple marry after Death

by SEAN O'SULLIVAN

Long ago there was a boy and a girl and they were in love with each other. They had been walking out together for five or six years and the boy had promised to marry her. That was all right until a second girl came home from America. She had a good lot of money, and didn't the boy turn his back on the first girl and go about with the other. When the first girl saw what was happening, she became heart-broken and died. That was that. Before the day on which he was to marry the second girl came, some kind of sickness came on him and he died.

Seven years after that there was a wedding in the next townland, and all the local boys and girls went to it. A young man was on his way to the wedding at night, and his shoes needed mending. He went to the house of a shoemaker at the side of the street and asked him would he mend his shoes.

'I will. Take them off,' said the shoemaker.

He slipped off the shoes, and it was late at night by the time they were mended. He set out then for the wedding-house. He took a short-cut by the side of a hill. The night was fine and bright.

He saw a white ghost coming down the hill towards him, and he stopped to look. When the ghost came near him at the other side of a fence, the young man asked him was he dead or alive.

'I'm dead,' said the ghost.

'What's wrong that you are like this?'

'I'll be like this forever until I marry the girl I promised to marry in this world,' said the ghost. 'I have been dead for seven years and have been going about like this ever since. I was engaged to a girl before I died but I broke my promise to her and went with another girl. The first girl died of a broken heart, and I died before I could marry the other one. I'll be going round like this forever unless I get someone from this world to stand sponsor for me at my marriage in the next world. Will you do that?'

'I will!'

The ghost left him and it wasn't long before a kind of sleep came over the young man beside the fence. He awoke to find himself at the edge of a cliff. He saw an island in the sea in front of him. Sleep came over him again and when he awoke he found himself on the island. He stood up and remembered his promise to stand sponsor at a wedding. He saw a chapel some distance away and he went towards it. He went in and sat on one of the seats. It wasn't long until a priest passed by him up along the chapel, and then he saw the white ghost following, with a girl at the other side. They didn't stop till they reached the altar. The priest went up on the altar, and the ghost and the girl went on their knees. The priest called out:

'Come up here, living man, and stand sponsor for these!'

He got up from the seat and went to the altar. The priest married them and then took them into a small room. The priest wrote down in a book that the pair were married, and the young man had to write with the pen that he had been sponsor.

'Now,' said the priest to the young man, 'when you go home, you must go to the parish priest and tell him that I have married such a couple in the other world. He won't believe you, but he will get it in his book!'

'I'm very thankful to you,' said the ghost. 'This is the girl I was to marry first, but we died. Your father knew this girl well.'

They left him. Sleep came over him once more, and he awoke at the foot of the hill where he had fallen asleep first. He stood up and went off towards the wedding-house, but it was almost over. He danced a little and took a drink and ate a bite; he was very hungry after the night. When he reached home, he told his father what had happened.

'Father,' he asked, 'was there a couple like that here who died?'

'There was. I knew them well.'

'I must go to the parish priest today to tell him that they are married,' said the son.

He went to the parish priest. The priest asked him what he wanted.

'This is what I want. Go to your book of marriages and see will you find the names of a certain couple in it.'

He told the priest their names.

'Don't be telling lies! It can't be true!' said the priest.

'It might be, father. I had to promise that I'd come to you to ask you to search your book for them.'

The priest got up and went to the marriage-book. He found their names there.

'You were right,' said he.

That's my story. If there's a lie in it, let it be! I heard it about fifty years ago from an old woman named Siobhán O'Sullivan, who lived in this townland. She was about fifty years old at that time.

(from *Legends from Ireland*)

The Death Coach

by T. CROFTON CROKER

'Tis midnight! — how gloomy and dark!
By Jupiter, there's not a star! —
'T is fearful! — 't is awful! — and hark!
What sound is that comes from afar?

Still rolling and rumbling, that sound
Makes nearer and nearer approach;
Do I tremble, or is it the ground? —
Lord, save us! — what is it? — a coach! —

A coach! but that coach has no head;
And the horses are headless as it;
Of the driver the same may be said,
And the passengers inside who sit.

See the wheels! how they fly o'er the stones!
And whirl, as the whip it goes crack:
Their spokes are of dead men's thigh-bones,
And the pole is the spine of the back!

The hammer-cloth, shabby display,
Is a pall rather mildew'd by damps;
And to light this strange coach on its way,
Two hollow skulls hang up for lamps!

From the gloom of Rathcooney church-yard,
  They dash down the hill of Glanmire;
    Pass Lota in gallop as hard
  As if horses were never to tire!

With people thus headless 't is fun
  To drive in such furious career;
Since *headlong* their horses can't run,
  Nor coachman be *headdy* from beer.

Very steep is the Tivoli lane,
But up-hill to them is as down;
Nor the charms of Woodhill can detain
These Dullahans rushing to town.

Could they feel as I've felt — in a song —
A spell that forbade them depart;
They'd a lingering visit prolong,
And after their head lose their heart!

No matter! — 't is past twelve o'clock;
Through the streets they sweep on like the wind,
And, taking the road to Blackrock,
Cork city is soon left behind.

Should they hurry thus reckless along,
To supper instead of to bed,
The landlord will surely be wrong,
If he charge it at so much a head!

Yet mine host may suppose them too poor
To bring to his wealth an increase;
As till now, all who drove to his door,
Possess'd at least *one crown* a-piece.

Up the Deadwoman's hill they are roll'd;
Boreenmannah is quite out of sight;
Ballintemple they reach, and behold!
At its church-yard they stop and alight.

'Who's there?' said a voice from the ground;
'We've no room, for the place is quite full.'
'Oh, room must be speedily found,
For we come from the parish of Skull.

THE DEATH COACH

'Though Murphys and Crowleys appear
   On headstones of deep-letter'd pride;
Though Scannels and Murleys lie here,
   Fitzgeralds and Toomies beside;

'Yet here for the night we lie down,
   To-morrow we speed on the gale;
For having no heads of our own,
   We seek the Old Head of Kinsale.'

(from *Fairy Legends & Traditions of the South of Ireland*)

Midnight Funeral from America

by SEAN O'SULLIVAN

Here's a story that I'm going to tell you now, and I promise you that there's no lie in it!

The man to whom this happened was from Connemara, from a place called Garumna. He emigrated to America, not too long ago at all. He had been there four or five years, and one night he went out to visit some Irish people who were living near him. He spent a good piece of the night with them, and then said that it was time for him to return to his lodgings.

When he left them, he was walking along the street and at a corner he saw a very large funeral coming towards him, carrying a coffin on their shoulders.

He had heard it always said in Ireland that one should not pass by a funeral without taking 'three steps of mercy' along with it. So he turned back and walked the three steps.

As he walked, the next thing he felt was that he was carried back to Ireland, to his own place in Garumna! The graveyard was very near his old home, so when the corpse was taken in there, he ran in to his own house. The door was closed, as if the people of the house had gone out visiting. At that time it was the custom to keep a pot of boiled potatoes beside the fire for anybody who might call to the house. There was a pot near the fire, and he went over to it and

121

took a handful of the hot potatoes. He then left the house; it was where his father and mother had lived, and where he himself was reared. He ate the potatoes and went into the graveyard.

'Now,' said he, 'this is where my father is buried here in Garumna. Isn't it strange what's happening to me tonight!';

He decided to visit his father's grave. There was a stone at its head, with his father's name and the date of his death. He knelt down and offered a Pater and Creed for his soul. He had a knife in his own pocket, with his name on it. He pulled out the knife, opened the blade and stuck it down beside the headstone where his father's head lay. He then went to where the corpse was being buried, and that was a hard job. When it was done, the people at the funeral left and he followed them. In less than an hour and a half or two hours at most from the time he had left America, he was back again at the place where he had met the funeral! The people of the funeral scattered, and he went off to the house where he was lodging. His great wonder was how far he had travelled during the night and all he had seen and done!

He went to work next day, and he found the day long till he came to his lodgings in the evening. He wrote a letter home to Ireland, giving his family the date of the day that he had met the funeral and gone to Ireland with it. He asked them had they been surprised when they came home that night that some potatoes had been taken out of the pot.

'Ye may not believe me, but it was I who was in the house that night and took the potatoes! And after that I went with a funeral that was burying a corpse in the graveyard, and I went to my father's grave and said a Pater and Creed for his soul. When I had done that, I put my hand in my pocket and took out a knife which had my name and surname on it. Go to the grave, and ye will find the knife standing beside the headstone over my father, if I'm not telling a lie! Write back to me and tell me is my story true or not!'

Very well. They received the letter. When they came home on the night he mentioned, everyone in the house had been surprised that some of the potatoes were missing. They had no notion, under the God of Graces, who took them. They went to the graveyard where their father's grave was, and found the knife with his name and surname on it stuck down beside the headstone. And he over in America!

I heard that story, and there's no lie in it. 'Tisn't long since it happened. The man was from Garumna. The dear blessing of God and of the Church on the souls of the dead, and may ourselves and all who are present be seventeen hundred thousand times better off, a year from tonight, and Amen!

(from *Legends from Ireland*)

The Demon Angler

by MERVYN WALL

I t's a queer thing. The visitors who come here are always full of talk about the 'other-worldliness' of Connemara. That's the expression they use — 'other-worldliness'; I've heard them myself. You'll see them any day of the summer standing over there in the hotel garden, men and women in their strange tourist clothes, staring down at the sea and at the rocks and the islands, or across at the hill on the far side of the bay. They'll even stop you to ask whether the seaweed in Connemara is always of a saffron colour, and they'll tell you that saffron seaweed stretching three miles along the inlet, is a most remarkable sight. But what seems to impress them most of all is the roads in the neighbourhood when the night is coming on. Many a time a visitor in his new golfing jacket has joined me walking home in the twilight, and told me that he feels the 'other-world' is close at hand, that the air is tremulous and pregnant with something about to happen, and that he understands the Irish belief in a world of faery. I remember one gentleman referring to the whole area as 'The Haunted Coast'.

We never contradict the tourists. After all, they're a quiet, well-behaved class of people, and I suppose their holiday costs them a lot of money. Moreover, they provide us with a lot of interest and amusement during the summer, and God knows it's dull enough in a Connemara village; but we haven't the leisure ourselves for notions of that sort, about the 'other-worldliness' of the locality. You don't have time for that class of thing when you're trying to scrape a living from two acres of grass and rock, or from the uneasy sea. When I say it's queer this talk visitors have of a haunted coast, I don't mean it's queer that they should have such ideas – after all I wouldn't expect strangers to have the same way of looking at things as the normal people of the countryside – but it's queer in this way, that the only genuine authenticated haunting we know of in this part of Connemara, is done, not by a creature from the faery world or even a deceased local, but by the ghost of a tourist himself – a draper's assistant from Capel Street, Dublin, by the name of Ambrose MacGrath.

I met him the first morning he was here: he came over from the hotel to speak to me where I was leaning over the wall smoking my pipe and looking down at the couple of row-boats in the harbour. He was a lanky young fellow dressed in navy blue, with a white unhealthy face; and he had a way of throwing his long legs about when he walked as if the hinges in his knees were loose.

He told me that he had arrived the night before for a fortnight's holiday, which he was going to spend in fishing for trout. He had never fished before, but the previous week in Dublin he had bought a rod, some casts and twenty-four flies as well as a net on a stick for landing the big ones. He also had four books on trout fishing in his suitcase. The girl in the hotel had pointed me out to him as the only angler in the village, and she had advised him to have a chat with me about the lakes and streams in the neighbourhood.

All the time he was talking he kept glancing over his shoulder, up and down the street, as if this was the queerest place he had ever set his foot in. Perhaps I should have told you that our village is just a row of whitewashed houses facing the sea. It straggles up the side of a hill as far as the church, and there it stops. After that, for sixteen gold miles until you come to Clifden, there's just the road, the rocky coast, the bogs and the mountains.

At last he asked me where the inhabitants were. He said he had been out already that morning and walked the length of the village. He had counted just over a hundred houses; but while there was the same number of dogs, one lying at the door of each house with its paws crossed, he hadn't seen a single human being. I explained that most of the people would hardly be up yet — it was scarcely ten o'clock. Of course, between ourselves, another reason why he didn't see anyone, is that we're a very well-bred village. I've heard that elsewhere in Ireland the people all come to their doors to look at a stranger. We'd never think of embarrassing a visitor like that — our people watch a stranger from behind the curtains until he is out of sight.

Mr. Ambrose MacGrath was depressed because when he arrived the night before, the first thing he learned was that this isn't a trout fishing area at all, but a centre for sea-fishing. There were two English gentlemen staying at the hotel, one of them no less than a lord; and in the usual friendly Irish fashion MacGrath had opened his book of flies on the diningroom table and started to chat about the fishing prospects. They had kept themselves very aloof and had given him to understand that they were there to fish for

Blue-nosed Shark, which are very plentiful off this coast. Later he saw the English lord coming through the yard carrying a twelve-inch hook on his shoulder — our friend thought at first it was a ship's anchor. That seems to have finished him. He slipped his little book of flies into his pocket and crept upstairs to bed.

While he told me this he kept staring at me with what I can only call resentment.

'I've always understood,' says he 'and the tourist literature that I've read, would seem to bear it out, that every bit of water in Connemara is leppin' with trout just dying to be caught.'

'I don't know how things may be in other parts,' I said, 'but to say that would be to exaggerate the position here. The fact is people just don't come here trout fishing at all. But you needn't be discouraged,' I added seeing how savage he was looking, 'there's two little lakes up the road beyond the church full of small trout, and in the bogs behind Errisbeg Mountain there's more lakes than you can count, and the trout there are large. I've fished every lake behind Errisbeg when I was a younger man, and you'll get plenty of sport there, tho' a city man like yourself may find it a bit wet underfoot.'

He cheered up considerably.

'I don't mind getting my feet wet,' says he. 'I brought plenty of pairs of socks with me,' and he explained that he was an assistant in the drapery business.

'I don't think you'll do so well to-day,' I said. 'The wind is in the north.'

He threw a queer look at me, and pulling a book out of his pocket he turned the pages until he came to a piece of poetry which he read half to himself and half to me:

> When the wind is in the north
> The wise angler fares not forth.

He began to look down-in-the-mouth again until I reminded

him that as he had never fished before he couldn't do better than spend his first day in the hotel garden practising casts. We went up there together, and I showed him how to tie on the flies and how to flip his wrist. I must say he was an apt pupil, and he did no damage except occasionally to whisk a piece of the hotel laundry off the clothes line. After a time the proprietress came out and asked us would we mind practising somewhere else. So along we went to the first lake beyond the church, and even though the wind was in the north we tried our hand there. He didn't catch anything, but I like to remember how happy he was that day walking back with me to the village. I think it was the only time I ever saw him happy.

The following day there was a thunderstorm, and of course that's ruinous – the trout just go to the bottom for a couple of days and bury their heads in the mud. After that the wind shifted to the east, and as one of his books told him that such conditions are 'neither good for man nor beast' Ambrose MacGrath didn't go out at all: he spent his time practising casts on the bit of waste ground down by the harbour, with all the children in the village

lined along the wall watching him. Every now and again he'd gather a handful of grass to throw up in the air so as to find out whether the wind was changing to a more favourable quarter. This amused the children, and soon they were all at it.

I remember that it exasperated him greatly when every evening after sunset the English lord and his friend would come into the harbour with the couple of shark they had caught, and have them heaved up on to the pier to be measured and weighed. They'd leave them there for an hour or so to be admired by everyone before throwing them back again into the water.

I think it was on the Saturday that Ambrose MacGrath was in my garden complaining bitterly that half his holiday was over, when he suddenly discovered that the wind had changed. 'When the wind is in the south,' says he, 'it blows the hook in the fish's mouth,' and off with him like a shot to the hotel to get his tackle.

But he wasn't content even then; he was annoyed at the fine weather: it irked him particularly that fish won't rise when the sun is in the sky. 'I'm expected,' he said bitterly, 'to creep out like a malefactor in the early morning or in the evening when the sun has gone down.' What matter but he always spoke as if I was personally responsible for the vagaries of nature. I'm a peaceful man, but when he'd sit there in my kitchen uninvited, and look at me with real hatred, it used rise my dander to think of this city shop-assistant who wasn't content to behave like a normal fisherman, but had such a mania for catching things. There almost at his door were two small lakes to wander round, rocks to scramble over to his heart's content, water to cast his flies in, and plenty of dry places to sit down and smoke his pipe. But no, he wasn't content: nothing would do him but he must catch a fish. I remember an evening he came in when I was sitting by the corner of the fire reading my way through the words of Sir Walter Scott, who must be the greatest writer in the world. I never saw a man that looked so black.

'There's a swan nesting on the lake,' says he.

'Well?' said I.

'Well indeed!' says he. 'How can I fish there? Every time I approach the edge the male bird comes rushing at me flapping its wings and disturbing all the trout.'

'There's the other little lake beyond,' I said.

'I can't get at the water there,' he says. 'There's ten yards of reeds all round it. I've lost five flies already.'

131

'Well,' said I, 'there's no use accusing me. I didn't make the country hereabouts.'

'I'm not accusing you,' he said very hot. 'I'm accusing Connemara,' and he muttered something about taking up the matter with the Tourist Board.

Seeing how put out he was I began to be sorry for him, so I promised to take the day off on the morrow and bring him up over Errisbeg to the great country of lakes beyond.

It was a nice cloudy day with the wind inclining to the west when we climbed the shoulder of the mountain and looked down at the three hundred and sixty-five lakes that are said to be in the twelve square miles of bog behind Errisbeg. He was excited at first, but when we started the descent he began complaining again.

'I didn't know you were going to lead me into a morass,' he says as he sank to his knees in the bog.

'If you exercised more judgment as to where you placed your feet,' I replied, 'you wouldn't get so wet. Can't you walk where the ground is firm, and jump from tuft to tuft like I do?'

He wasn't much good at that either, and he was thoroughly wet when we scrambled down to the edge of Lough Nalawney, but the sight of the stretch of water brightened him up, and he had his rod fixed in a jiffy. Then he started bothering me as to

what flies he should use. I always employ live bait myself. I kept flies at one time, but every winter the moths used eat them. At last he tied on a Wickham's Fancy and two other flies so brightly coloured that no trout would take them into his mouth except through wanton curiosity.

We fished the lake for a few hours, but when we sat down for something to eat he was at it again. He was a bit annoyed, I think, because I had taken a two-pounder while he had caught nothing.

'Look here,' says he. 'We'll say this lake is about a mile in cir-cumference.'

'Right,' I said prepared to concede anything.

'The fishing books,' says he, 'tell you that you should only fish the leeside of a lake. That reduces the length of shore that you can fish from, to about a third of a mile.'

'Well?' I said. 'What about it?'

'Of that third,' says he, 'the greatest part is taken up by reeds which you can't cast across or by boggy soil which prevents you approaching the water's edge. So it amounts to this, that in a lake of this size there are really only five or six places from which you can fish at all. And to make matters worse,' says he, 'they tell you that you must cast with the wind. That's impossible,' says he, 'because if you're on the leeside of the lake the wind is blowing in your face. The whole thing is a cod,' says he. 'It's impossible to catch fish. It's all a device to defraud tourists.'

'No doubt you're right,' I said putting the two-pounder into my bag. That annoyed him more, and I left him muttering to himself, and off I went to have a cast or two myself. I took three more small ones while he didn't even get a rise tho' he tried every fly in his repertoire. When I joined him again he looked sourly at my take, and pulling out a map he screwed at it for a minute or two. Then he said he was going across to Lough Rannaghan. I tried to dissuade him — it was about a mile away across the bogs, and it's easy enough to get lost in that waste bit of country, especially with the evening coming on. But nothing would do him but to try his luck over there. I heard afterwards that he was out all night and with no luck either.

I didn't see him for a few days after that, but I heard from the girl in the hotel that he had written to Dublin for a pair of waders and a fresh consignment of flies of every known pattern. He hadn't a single trout to his credit yet and had become so short-tempered that everyone in the hotel was afraid to speak to him. Each evening he was off across the mountain, fished all the night through and returned to the hotel for breakfast. Then he went to bed to sleep or to read more books dealing with the psychology of the trout, which were arriving for him by every post. The girl in the hotel

complained of the mess he had his room in, casts steeping in the water jug and the like; and she said that she couldn't make his bed or touch any of his clothes, even his pyjamas, without getting a hook embedded in her hand. I think the hotel people were looking forward as much as I was to the day when he'd return to his counter-jumping in Capel Street, Dublin, but I declare to goodness on the Saturday there he was at my gate with a rod in his hand and a circle of flies around his hat.

'I got a rise last night,' he said with a glitter in his eye. 'At Lough Nelawney.'

'Did you now?' I said. 'That's very encouraging.'

'He took it into his mouth,' says he, 'but he spat it out again before I could strike. I think he must have been a big one by the force he employed in spitting out the fly.'

'Too bad,' I said, 'that you must return to Dublin to-day or to-morrow.'

He threw a crafty look at me. 'I'm not going back,' he says. 'I'm staying another week.'

'But what about your job?' I asked.

'I've a pain in my chest,' says he. 'I've been up to see the doctor, and he's given me a certificate. I've just posted it on to the firm.'

The month of August passed. Every week Ambrose MacGrath was up to the doctor. Poor old Doctor Maguire was sorely puzzled. He couldn't find anything wrong with MacGrath, but he had to take the patient's word for the pain. To make it more difficult the pain kept moving. The doctor followed it from MacGrath's chest round to the small of his back. It was six weeks later that the drapery firm in Dublin gave MacGrath the sack.

He didn't mind: he hadn't caught a trout yet, and he was now spending eighteen hours out of twenty-four at Lough Nalawney. Anxious and bitter letters kept arriving from his wife. He left them lying round the hotel so that soon the whole village knew that the wife and children had to leave their home because he wouldn't pay the rent. All his money went to buy a new rod, whole parcels of books on the life history of the trout, cases of flies and an extraordinary new suit of the colour and texture of grass.

'Have you ever studied background?' he says to me when he came to show me the new suit.

'I beg your pardon,' said I.

'I know now,' he says, 'the reason for my lack of success. I've been reading all about background. The eye of the trout

distinguishes sharply between colours, and if he sees a bit of navy blue moving against a background of green, he knows there's something up. You have to merge into your background. At Lough Nalawney the background is mostly long unhealthy looking grass. This is the nearest I could get to it in a suit. What do you think of it?' He turned round so that I could admire the back.

'It's like what the farmers call "silage",' I said. 'It's like a haystack only that it's green.'

He began telling me how he'd start fifty yards from the edge of the lake and crawl through the grass so quietly that the fish would think he was a bit of the bank. I listened, but all the time I was thinking of the wife and children without a roof over their heads, and the vacant place behind the draper's counter. He went on to tell me of a cannibal trout, a monster of about twenty pounds, that he had sighted running itself in the shallows at the edge of Lough Nalawney. For a solid hour he had held a Wickham's Fancy within an inch of its nose. Four times the trout had opened its mouth, and MacGrath had nearly fallen into the lake with the excitement. The fifth time it opened its mouth it came to him suddenly that the fish was only yawning, and in spite of the agonising pains he was suffering in his right arm he had tried to flick the fly down its throat, but the monster had turned and darted away into deep water. But he wasn't discouraged. He was determined to catch that particular trout,

and he wasn't going to leave the village until he had it landed.

The people here considered him a bit cracked, but they didn't pay much heed, because they knew that all tourists are queer; and none of us began really worrying about him until his determination to merge into his background made him paint his face and his hands green. It was late in September, and tho' he still hadn't caught a single fish, he had twice sighted the same monster trout in Lough Nalawney. He had got it into his head that the other fish which jumped in the lake, did so to distract his attention from the pursuit of this grandfather of all the trout, and I believe that even if he had succeeded in catching any number of smaller ones, he wouldn't have been satisfied. No one ever went with him on his nightly journeyings across Errisbeg, and I don't blame them: I wouldn't have cared to go myself, keen angler tho' I am. It's a lonely spot to be with a fellow the like of that, a place where you wouldn't even have the company of your own shadow until the moon came up over the bogs.

After he painted himself green a few of us met one evening in the Atlantic Bar to talk it over and discuss whether we shouldn't start doing something about it. We thought of going up to the priest's house and asking Father James to talk to him. But we were too late: the following morning MacGrath didn't come back to the hotel, nor did he come during the day; and it was just coming on for nightfall when we found him. He had caught the monster trout, or maybe I should say that it had caught him. It had pulled him in. What grappling in the water up and down the lake the two of them had, no one will ever know. We found him drowned in the reeds with the twenty-pounder on his line.

It was a great sin he had committed against his wife and children, and no one can say but that he deserved his punishment. Maybe it was allowed to happen as a warning to the desperate fishermen you sometimes meet, who knows? Everyone spoke bad of him: I was the only one that tried to say a good word, because I'm an angler myself, and I know what it is when it gets

its grip on you.

It wasn't long until stories began to be whispered round the neighbourhood, and soon it came to be thought unlucky for anyone, above all for an angler, to go near Lough Nalawney. First, a man herding his sheep across the side of Errisbeg saw from a distance something moving among the rocks beside the lake. Then there were others.

I know for myself, tho' I'm as mad about fishing as any man, I content myself with the two small lakes beyond the church. Nothing in this world would make me cross the ridge of Errisbeg of an evening. It's a ghostly place, Lough Nalawney, with no sound except the breeze stirring the grass among the rocks at the water's edge. Go and look at it yourself, but go in the day time when the sun is high over the bogs, and don't let anything on this earth persuade you to loiter there when it comes on towards evening and the sun goes down.

(from *A Flutter of Wings*)

The Ghost in Graigue

by PATRICK KENNEDY

A lady in the neighbourhood of that old town, much celebrated for her charities, died, and great sorrow was felt
for her loss. Many masses were celebrated, and many
prayers offered up for the repose of her soul, and there was a
moral certainty of her salvation among her acquaintance.

One evening, after the family had retired to rest, a servant
girl in the house, a great favourite with her late mistress, was
sitting beside the fire, enjoying the dreamy comfort of a hard-
worked person after the day's fatigues, and just before the utter
forgetfulness of sleep. Her mind was wandering to her late loved
mistress, when she was startled by a sensation in her instep, as if
it were trodden upon.

'Bad manners to you for a dog,' said she, suspecting the 'collie'
of the house to be the offender.

But to her great terror, when she looked down and round the
hearth, she could see no living thing.

'Who's that?' she cried out, with the teeth chattering in her
head.

'It is I,' was the answer, and the dead lady became visible to her.

'Oh, mistress darling!' said she. 'What is disturbing you, and can
I do anything for you?'

'You can do a little,' said the spirit, 'and that is the reason I
have appeared to you. Every day and every hour some one of my
friends is lamenting me, and speaking of my goodness, and that is

tormenting me in the other world. All my charities were done only for the pleasure of having myself spoken well of, and they are now prolonging my punishment. The only real good I ever did was to give, once, half-a-crown to a poor scholar that was studying to be a priest, and charging him to say nothing about it. That was the only good act that followed me into the other world. And now you must tell my husband and my children to speak well of my past life no more, or I will haunt you night after night.'

The appearance, the next moment, was no longer there, and the poor girl fainted the moment it vanished. When she recovered, she hastened into her settle-bed, and covered herself up, head and all, and cried and sobbed till morning.

Everyone wondered the next day to see such a troubled countenance. But she went through her business one way or other, though she could not make up her mind to tell her master what she had seen and heard. She dreaded the quiet hour of rest; and well she might, for the displeased lady visited her again at the same hour, and reproached her for her neglect.

Three times she endured the dread visits before she made the required revelation.

(from *Legendary Fictions of the Irish Celts*)

Legend of the Banshee

by T. CROFTON CROKER

The Reverend Charles Bunworth was rector of Buttevant, in the county of Cork, about the middle of the last century. He was a man of unaffected piety and of sound learning, pure in heart and benevolent in intention. By the rich he was respected, and by the poor beloved; nor did a difference of creed prevent their looking up to *'the minister'* (so was Mr. Bunworth called by them) in matters of difficulty and in seasons of distress, confident of receiving from him the advice and assis-

tance that a father would afford to his children. He was the friend and the benefactor of the surrounding country; to him, from the neighbouring town of Newmarket, came both Curran and Yelverton for advice and instruction, previous to their entrance at Dublin College. Young indigent and inexperienced, these afterwards eminent men received from him, in addition to the advice they sought, pecuniary aid, and the brilliant career which was theirs justified the discrimination of the giver.

But what extended the fame of Mr. Bunworth far beyond the limits of the parishes adjacent to his own was his performance on the Irish harp, and his hospitable reception and entertainment of the poor harpers who travelled from house to house about the

country. Grateful to their patron, these itinerant minstrels sang his praises to the tingling accompaniment of their harps, invoking in return for his bounty abundant blessings on his white head, and celebrating in their rude verses the blooming charms of his daughters, Elizabeth and Mary. It was all these poor fellows could do; but who can doubt that their gratitude was sincere when, at the time of Mr. Bunworth's death, no less than fifteen harps were deposited in the loft of his granary, bequeathed to him by the last members of a race which has now ceased to exist. Trifling, no doubt, in intrinsic value were these relics, yet there is something in gifts of the heart that merits preservation, and it is to be regretted that, when he died, these harps were broken up one after the other, and used as firewood by an ignorant follower of the family, who, on their removal to Cork for a temporary change of scene, was left in charge of the house.

The circumstances attending the death of Mr. Bunworth may be doubted by some; but there are still living credible witnesses who declare their authenticity, and who can be produced to attest most, if not all, of the following particulars.

About a week previous to his dissolution, and early in the evening, a noise was heard at the hall door resembling the shearing of sheep; but at the time no particular attention was paid to it. It was nearly eleven o'clock the same night when Kavanagh, the herdsman, returned from Mallow, whither he had been sent in the afternoon for some medicine, and was observed by Miss Bunworth, to whom he delivered the parcel, to be much agitated. At this time, it must be observed, her father was by no means considered in danger.

'What is the matter, Kavanagh?' asked Miss Bunworth; but the poor fellow, with a bewildered look, only uttered: 'The master, Miss — the master — he is going from us?' and overcome with real grief, he burst into a flood of tears.

Miss Bunworth, who was a woman of strong nerve, inquired if anything he had learned in Mallow induced him to suppose that her father was worse.

'No, miss,' said Kavanagh; 'it was not in Mallow —'

'Kavanagh,' said Miss Bunworth, with that stateliness of manner for which she is said to have been remarkable, 'I fear you have been drinking, which, I must say, I did not expect at such a time as the present, when it was your duty to have kept yourself sober; I thought you might have been trusted. What should we have done if you had broken the medicine bottle or lost it? For the doctor said it was of the greatest consequence that your master should take the medicine to-night. But I

will speak to you in the morning, when you are in a fitter state to understand what I say.'

Kavanagh looked up with a stupidity of aspect which did not serve to remove the impression of his being drunk, as his eyes appeared heavy and dull after the flood of tears; but his voice was not that of an intoxicated person.

'Miss,' said he, 'as I hope to receive mercy hereafter, neither bit nor sup has passed my lips since I left this house; but the master —'

'Speak softly,' said Miss Bunworth; 'he sleeps, and is going on as well as we could expect.'

'Praise be to God for that, anyway,' replied Kavanagh; 'but oh! miss, he is going from us surely — we will lose him — the master — we will lose him, we will lose him!' and he wrung his hands together.

'What is it you mean, Kavanagh?' asked Miss Bunworth.

'I mean,' said Kavanagh; the Banshee has come for him, miss; and 'tis not I alone who have heard her.'

''Tis an idle superstition,' said Miss Bunworth.

'Maybe so,' replied Kavanagh, as if the words 'idle superstition' only sounded upon his ear without reaching his mind — 'Maybe so,' he continued; 'but as I came through the glen of Ballybeg, she was along with me keening and screeching, and clapping her hands by my side, every step of the way, with her long white hair falling about her shoulders, and I could hear her repeat the master's name every now and then, as plain as ever I heard it. When I came to the old abbey, she parted from me there, and turned into the pigeon-field next the *berrin*' ground, and folding her cloak about her, down she sat under the tree that was struck by the lightning, and began keening so bitterly, that it went through one's heart to hear it.'

'Kavanagh,' said Miss Bunworth, who had, however, listened attentively to this remarkable relation, 'my father is, I believe, better; and I hope will himself soon be up and able to convince you that all this is but your own fancy; nevertheless, I charge you not to mention what you have told me, for there is no occasion to frighten your fellow-servants with the story.'

Mr. Bunworth gradually declined; but nothing particular occurred until the night previous to his death: that night both his daughters, exhausted with continued attendance and watching, were prevailed upon to seek some repose; and an elderly lady, a near relative and friend of the family, remained by the bedside of their father. The old gentleman then lay in the parlour, where he had been in

the morning removed at his own request, fancying the change would afford him relief; and the head of his bed was placed close to the window. In a room adjoining sat some male friends, and, as usual on like occasions of illness, in the kitchen many of the followers of the family had assembled.

The night was serene and moonlit — the sick man slept — and nothing broke the stillness of their melancholy watch, when the little party in the room adjoining the parlour, the door of which stood open, was suddenly roused by a sound at the window near the bed. A rose-tree grew outside the window, so close as to touch the glass; this was forced aside with some noise, and a low moaning was heard, accompanied by clapping of hands, as if of a female in deep affliction. It seemed as if the sound proceeded from a person holding her mouth close to the window. The lady who sat by the bedside of Mr. Bunworth went into the adjoining room, and in a tone of alarm inquired of the gentlemen there if they had heard the Banshee? Sceptical of supernatural appearances, two of them rose hastily and went out to discover the cause of these sounds, which they also had distinctly heard. They walked all round the house, examining every spot of ground, particularly near the window from whence the voice had proceeded; the bed of earth beneath, in which the rose-tree was planted, had been recently dug, and the print of a footstep — if the tree had been forced aside by mortal hand — would have inevitably remained; but they could perceive no such impression; and an unbroken stillness reigned without. Hoping to dispel the mystery, they continued their search anxiously along the road, from the straightness of which, and the lightness of the night, they were enabled to see some distance around them; but all was silent and deserted, and they returned surprised and disappointed. How much more, then, were they astonished at learning that the whole time of their absence, those who remained within the house had heard the moaning and clapping of hands even louder and more distinct than before they had gone out; and no sooner was the door of the room closed on them,

than they again heard the same mournful sounds! Every succeeding hour the sick man became worse, and as the first glimpse of the morning appeared, Mr. Bunworth expired.

(from *Legends and Tales of Ireland*)

Fior Usga

by T. CROFTON CROKER

A little way beyond the Gallows Green of Cork, and just outside the town, there is a great lough of water, where people
in the winter go and skate for the sake of diversion; but the
sport above the water is nothing to what is under it, for at the very
bottom of this lough there are buildings and gardens far more
beautiful than any now to be seen; and how they came there was
in this manner:

Long before Saxon foot
pressed Irish ground there
was a great king called
Corc, whose palace stood
where the lough now is,
in a round green valley,
that was just a mile
about. In the middle of
the courtyard was a spring
of fair water, so pure and
so clear that it was the
wonder of all the world.
Much did the king rejoice
at having so great a curios-

ity within his palace; but as people came in crowds from far and
near to draw the precious water of this spring, he was sorely
afraid that in time it might become dry; so he caused a high wall

to be built up round it, and would allow nobody to have the water, which was a very great loss to the poor people living about the palace. Whenever he wanted any for himself, he would send his daughter to get it, not liking to trust his servants with the key of the well-door, fearing that they might give some away.

One night the King gave a grand entertainment, and there were many great princes present, and lords and nobles without end; and there were wonderful doings throughout the palace: there were bonfires, whose blaze reached up to the very sky; and dancing was there, to such sweet music that it ought to have waked up the dead out of their graves, and feasting was there in the greatest of plenty for all who came; nor was anyone turned away from the palace gates, but 'You're welcome — you're welcome, heartily,' was the porter's salute for all.

Now, it happened at this grand entertainment there was one young prince above all the rest mighty comely to behold, and as tall and as stright as ever eye would wish to look on. Right merrily did he dance that night with the old king's daughter, wheeling here and wheeling there, as light as a feather, and footing it away to the admiration of everyone. The musicians played the better for seeing their dancing; and they danced as if their lives depended upon it. After all this dancing came the supper, and the young prince was seated at table by the side of his beautiful partner, who smiled upon him as often as he spoke to her; and that was by no means so often as he wished, for he had constantly to turn to the company and thank them for the many compliments passed upon his fair partner and himself.

In the midst of the banquet, one of the great lords said to King Corc: 'May it please your Majesty, here is everything in abundance that heart can wish for, both to eat and drink, except water.'

'Water!' said the King, mightily pleased at someone calling for that of which purposely there was a want. 'Water shall you have, my lord, speedily, and that of such a delicious kind, that I challenge all the world to equal it. Daughter,' said he, 'go fetch some in the golden vessel which I caused to be made for the purpose.'

The King's daughter, who was called Fior Usga (which signifies, in English, Spring Water), did not much like to be told to perform so menial a service before so many people, and though she did not venture to refuse the commands of her father, yet hesitated to obey him, and looked down upon the ground. The King, who loved his daughter very much, seeing this, was sorry for what he had desired her to do, but having said the word, he was never known to recall it; he therefore thought of a way to make his daughter go speedily and fetch the water, and it was by proposing that the young prince her partner should go along with her. Accordingly, with a loud voice, he said: 'Daughter, I wonder not at your fearing to go alone so late at night; but I doubt not

the young prince at your side will go with you.' The prince was not displeased at hearing this; and taking the golden vessel in one hand, with the other led the king's daughter out of the hall so gracefully that all present gazed after them with delight.

When they came to the spring of water in the court-yard of the palace, the fair Usga unlocked the door with the greatest care, and stooping down with the golden vessel to take some of the water out of the well, found the vessel so heavy that she lost her balance and fell in. The young prince tried in vain

to save her, for the water rose and rose so fast that the entire courtyard was speedily covered with it, and he hastened back almost in a state of distraction to the King.

The door of the well being left open, the water, which had been so long confined, rejoiced at obtaining its liberty, rushed forth incessantly, every moment rising higher and higher, and was in the hall of the entertainment sooner than the young prince himself, so that when he attempted to speak to the king he was up to his neck in water. At length the water rose to such a height that it filled the whole of the green valley in which the king's palace stood, and so the present lough of Cork was formed.

Yet the King and his guests were not drowned, as would now happen if such an awful inundation were to take place; neither was his daughter, the fair Usga, who returned to the banquet-hall the very next night after this dreadful event; and every night since the same entertainment and dancing goes on in the palace at the bottom of the lough, and will last until someone has the luck to bring up out of it the golden vessel which was the cause of all this mischief.

Nobody can doubt that it was a judgment upon the King for his shutting up the well in the courtyard from the poor people; and if there are any who do not credit my story, they may go and see the lough of Cork, for there it is to be seen to this day; the road to Kinsale passes at one side of it; and when its waters are low and clear, the tops of towers and stately buildings may be plainly viewed in the bottom by those who have good eyesight, without the help of spectacles.

(from *Legends and Tales of Ireland*)